"You mentioned terms. What did you have in mind?"

Laura lifted her chin and gave Kyle a shy smile. "I need an administrator."

Kyle shook his head. "Undercover means inconspicuous. If I come in as head honcho, every person at the institute will scrutinize the daylights out of me."

Laura sank down, shoulders slumped. "It seemed like the solution to both our problems."

Kyle settled beside her, longing to pull her into his arms and comfort her. He kept his distance. His reassuring hug might turn into something deeper. Wilder. "Just hire me as a simple researcher and let me start right away."

Laura turned to face him again, her expression calm and resolute. "There's one way to both get what we want."

Kyle smiled at her earnestness. "If you've thought of a solution, you're a miracle worker."

"It will work, all right." Her solemn eyes sought and held his gaze. "You'll have to marry me."

Dear Reader,

This holiday season, deck the halls with some of the most exciting names in romantic suspense: Anne Stuart *and* Gayle Wilson. These two award-winning authors have returned together to Harlequin Intrigue to reprise their much loved miniseries—CATSPAW and MEN OF MYSTERY—in a special 2-in-1 collection. *Night and Day* is a guaranteed keeper and the best stocking stuffer around!

Find out what happens when a single-dad secret agent has to protect a beautiful scientist as our MONTANA CONFIDENTIAL series continues with *Licensed To Marry* by Charlotte Douglas.

The *stork* is coming down the chimney this year, as Joanna Wayne begins a brand-new series of books set in the sultry South. Look for *Another Woman's Baby* this month and more HIDDEN PASSIONS books to come in the near future.

Also available from Harlequin Intrigue is the second title in Susan Kearney's HIDE AND SEEK trilogy. The search goes on in *Hidden Hearts*.

Happy holidays from all of us at Harlequin Intrigue.

Sincerely,

Denise O'Sullivan
Associate Senior Editor
Harlequin Intrigue

P.S.—Next month you can find *another* special holiday title—*A Woman with a Mystery* by B.J. Daniels

LICENSED
TO MARRY
CHARLOTTE DOUGLAS

HARLEQUIN®

TORONTO • NEW YORK • LONDON
AMSTERDAM • PARIS • SYDNEY • HAMBURG
STOCKHOLM • ATHENS • TOKYO • MILAN • MADRID
PRAGUE • WARSAW • BUDAPEST • AUCKLAND

Special thanks and acknowledgment are given
to Charlotte Douglas for her contribution
to the MONTANA CONFIDENTIAL series.

ISBN 0-373-22638-1

LICENSED TO MARRY

ABOUT THE AUTHOR

Charlotte Douglas has loved a good story since learning to read at the age of three. After years of teaching that love of books to her students, she now enjoys creating stories of her own. Often her books are set in one of her three favorite places: Montana, where she and her husband spent their honeymoon; the mountains of North Carolina, where they're building a summer home; and Florida, near the Gulf of Mexico on Florida's West Coast, where she's lived most of her life.

Books by Charlotte Douglas

HARLEQUIN INTRIGUE

HARLEQUIN AMERICAN ROMANCE

*Identity Swap

Don't miss any of our special offers. Write to us at the following address for information on our newest releases.

Harlequin Reader Service
U.S.: 3010 Walden Ave., P.O. Box 1325, Buffalo, NY 14269
Canadian: P.O. Box 609, Fort Erie, Ont. L2A 5X3

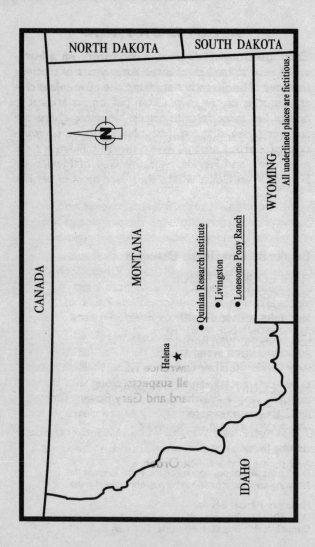

NORTH DAKOTA

SOUTH DAKOTA

All underlined places are fictitious.

WYOMING

CANADA

MONTANA

• Quinlan Research Institute
• Livingston
• Lonesome Pony Ranch

★ Helena

IDAHO

CAST OF CHARACTERS

Laura Quinlan—She's determined to expose the terrorists who have threatened her father's work, but is she willing to risk her heart as well as her life?

Kyle Foster—As a bomb demolition expert, he'll do whatever it takes to stop the Black Order from killing others, even if it means marrying a woman he has no intention of loving.

Molly Foster—Kyle's adorable three-year-old daughter.

Josiah Quinlan—Laura's father has developed the Quinlan Research Institute for the purpose of finding vaccines and antidotes against biological weapons.

Montana Confidential Covert Operations Group—Headed by Daniel Austin. Frank Connolly and Court Brady work with Kyle from their headquarters at the Lonesome Pony Ranch in their fight against the Black Order terrorists.

The Quinlan Research Institute Staff— When biological weapons end up in the hands of the Black Order, doctors Lawrence Tyson, Melinda Kwan and Robert Potter are all suspects, along with lab assistants Wayne Pritchard and Gary Bowen. Only Dr. C. J. Connolly, Frank's wife, is in the clear.

U.S. Senator Ross Weston—A presidential candidate running on an antiterrorism platform, he becomes a chief target of the Black Order.

Chapter One

On a bright September morning, Kyle Foster raced toward his worst nightmare.

Kicking gravel in his wake, he crossed the driveway, Stetson clutched to his head with one hand, in his other his toolkit banged against his thigh. With natural fluid grace and impressive strength from tough physical conditioning, he sprinted toward the waiting helicopter in the pasture. Determination glinted in his jade-green eyes and hardened the set of his square jaw.

He ducked beneath the spinning rotors and grasped the strong hand of Daniel Austin, who pulled him aboard just as the craft lifted into the air. Kyle removed his hat, stowed his kit beneath his seat, settled his headset over his ears and looked down at the Lonesome Pony Ranch, shrinking below him as the chopper gained altitude.

Molly, his three-year-old daughter, waved to him from the arms of Dale McMurty, the ranch's cook and Molly's surrogate grandmother. His gut cramped with fear when he thought of Molly with her mischievous eyes, green like his own, and masses of white-blond curls, whose plump face dimpled when she laughed, making even the toughest ranch hand smile. Deserted by her mother, she depended on Kyle for everything. There was no way he could botch this job and not come home to her.

Home.

Their snug cabin at the Lonesome Pony Ranch was home now. He and Molly had left the rush and turmoil of Los Angeles for the peace and quiet of Montana Yellowstone country, but the Lonesome Pony was not as serene as it appeared on the surface. The helicopter banked toward the western mountain range and Helena, and Kyle gazed at the deceptive landscape beneath him. Still resembling its former incarnation as a dude resort, the main house over-looked the pasture they had taken off from.

Beyond the pasture ran Crooked Creek, teeming with life, a fly fisherman's paradise. On the other side of the ranch house glistened the turquoise blue of the swimming pool, ringed with cabins, including the one where he and Molly lived. Farther from the house sat the massive barn and corrals, and behind them, archery and shooting ranges and a rodeo corral.

A casual, even a close-at-hand observer could not discern the secret operations room, deep beneath the main house. Ostensibly a retirement and breeding ranch for horses, the ranch served as a cover and headquarters for the covert agents of Montana Confidential, founded by Daniel Austin.

Kyle glanced at Daniel, sitting grim-faced in the seat beside him. In his mid-forties with sun-bleached blond hair and brown eyes framed with laugh lines,

Daniel had the rugged good looks of a film star who becomes more handsome with age. But his boss was far more than an attractive face. A Texas Confidential agent for more than fifteen years, Daniel had put together the secret Montana group at the request of the Department of Public Safety. Their main purpose was to ferret out international terrorists believed operating in the state.

Daniel returned Kyle's gaze. "Got everything you need?" his boss's rich voice asked through the headset.

Swallowing the panic that threatened to well into his throat, Kyle nodded and tapped his kit with the heel of his boot. "Got all my tools. I'll have to borrow body gear from the local bomb squad."

"You'll do fine." Daniel nodded in encouragement, and the compassion in his deep brown eyes spoke volumes.

More than the other agents, Daniel understood the crossroads at which Kyle found himself, because Daniel knew the whole story. While the others regarded Kyle as the hero who had saved the Beverly Hills Hotel from destruction three years ago, Daniel knew the darker side of Kyle's past: today would be the first bomb Kyle would face since his partner on the L.A. bomb squad had been blown to bits before his eyes.

In a habitual gesture, Kyle rubbed the crescent-shaped scar that intersected his left eyebrow and felt the old wounds tighten across his chest. If he lived to be a thousand, he'd never forget that horrific day—or expunge his own guilt. His hands shook slightly, and he gripped his knees to hide his nervousness. Now others were counting on him.

Including Daniel and his two new partners, sitting in the seats in front of him.

Frank Connolly handled the chopper with the steady confidence and skill of a career military pilot. He still suffered twinges from the injury to his right knee, but if he experienced any qualms about flying after being shot down over Bosnia, Kyle couldn't tell it from the skillful way Frank flew the helicopter. Only the slight tightening and flexing of his hands on the controls betrayed his tension. The chopper, supposedly at the ranch for patrolling fences and herding livestock, had its true purpose activated today: rapid deployment of the agents in emergency situations.

"What's our ETA?" Daniel asked.

Frank spoke into his mike without taking his eyes from the terrain below. "Fifteen minutes to Helena."

"Cutting it close." Daniel looked to Kyle.

Kyle shrugged with a nonchalance he didn't feel. "From what the capitol police told us, they can't read the timer on the bomb. We don't know how long we have."

"Let's hope we arrive in time for you to do your stuff, hotshot," Court Brody spoke from the copilot's chair.

A few weeks earlier, Kyle would have taken Court's comment as sarcasm. An FBI agent who had been assigned to the Montana Confidentials against his wishes, immediately upon his arrival Court had made clear his reluctance to be there. But after recently discovering he was a father and reuniting with his child's mother, he had decided to stay in Montana and quit the FBI and join the Confidential team. Like Frank, Court appeared unflappable, but Kyle knew better. The tiny muscle ticking in Court's jaw telegraphed his raw nerves. None of them knew what they were walking into.

Or if they'd walk out of it alive.

"Yeah," Frank chimed in, his voice calm, steady. "If anyone can keep that monster from blowing the capitol to smithereens, you can do it, Kyle, old buddy."

Court turned and grinned. "Hope you handle a bomb better than you do a horse, greenhorn."

"Maybe I should give you bomb duty, cowboy," Kyle joked back. "You could just lasso the damn thing. That's how they do it in Montana, isn't it?"

"That's right." Court's eyes twinkled. "Or I could just shoot it."

Their exchange of gallows humor helped, and Kyle settled back in his seat and tried to ease his residual anxiety by deep, steady breathing. He wished he felt the confidence the other members of the team had in him, but he couldn't stop blaming himself for Buzz Williams's death. Every second of that horrible day was etched indelibly in his brain. The memories made his gut cramp and his hands shake, a fatal problem for a bomb-disposal expert.

He and Buzz had answered the call at the Hollywood Bowl hours before a rock concert. A groundskeeper had discovered the explosive device only minutes before, and while the uniformed officers cleared and cordoned off the area, Kyle and Buzz had studied the bomb.

"It's sophisticated," Buzz said. "Nothing I ever saw before."

Kyle nodded in agreement. "Better back off and let me handle this one, kid."

"It's my turn."

"This is something new. I'd better do it."

Buzz shook his head. "It's as new to you as it is to me. Besides, how will I ever get experience if I don't take a shot at it?"

At the earnest pleading in Buzz's boyish face, Kyle relented. "Just take it by the book, okay? And holler if you need me."

Kyle moved a safe distance away, but not so far he couldn't observe Buzz's work. Seconds ticked away like anxiety-filled hours, and Buzz lifted his head and caught Kyle's eye. From that one look, Kyle knew the young man was in trouble, and he trundled toward him as fast as he could move in the cumbersome bodysuit.

He had covered only a few yards when the bomb blew.

Mercifully, the concussion of the blast knocked him unconscious, and he was carried away to a hospital before he ever regained his senses. He never saw what the bomb had done to young Buzz Williams.

But he could imagine.

And he could never forget the panic in Buzz's eyes seconds before the blast. In that instant, his young partner had known he was a dead man.

Kyle shook his head, trying to jostle the memories

loose. If anyone died today, it would be him. He glanced at his watch. Ten minutes to Helena. He prayed silently they would make it in time. Daniel had already advised the Helena bomb squad to back off. Kyle was the most experienced professional available, and if he couldn't defuse the terrorist bomb, no one could. He was damn good at demolition, he reminded himself.

If he could stop his hands from shaking.

IN THE ANTEROOM to the Montana governor's office in the capitol building, Laura Quinlan reached toward her father on the sofa beside her and flicked a speck of lint from the lapel of his best suit.

Josiah Quinlan, still vigorous and handsome at age seventy, thanked her with a loving smile. "Your mother, God rest her soul, used to do that whenever I'd get all gussied up for an important meeting. She always wanted me to look my best."

Laura hooked her arm through his with an affectionate squeeze. "You look terrific, Dad." She nodded toward the portfolio on his other side. "And with the test results you've brought to show him, the governor will have a hard time turning down your request."

Josiah eased a finger beneath his collar. "I'm a scientist, not a fund-raiser. I wish things like this didn't keep me from my work."

Noting the hint of shadows beneath his eyes, Laura felt her heart clench with concern. "You work too hard. It's about time you took a day off."

"A day off." He snorted with good humor. "I'd

rather work forty hours straight in the lab than face someone, hat in hand, asking for financial support.''

Laura nodded, sharing her father's frustration. ''With the threat of terrorists with biological weapons, you'd think the federal government would provide all the funding you need, without us having to beg, borrow or steal to keep our vaccine research—''

''Dr. Quinlan, Miss Quinlan,'' the secretary interrupted. ''The governor will see you now.''

Josiah pushed to his feet, straightened his coat and gave Laura a look as if he were off to face a firing squad. ''Here goes.''

''Relax, Daddy.'' She rose and handed him his portfolio. ''You'll do fine.''

He squeezed her hand. ''I'm glad you'll be in there pitching with me, sugar. We make a good team.''

She preceded her father into the adjoining office. Governor Harry Haskel stood behind his massive mahogany desk to greet them.

''Josiah, you old dog,'' the handsome politician said with a grin the media cameras loved and an approving glance at Laura. ''You never told me what a beauty your daughter is.''

Haskel skirted his desk and offered Laura a chair with old-fashioned gallantry. Determined not to spoil her father's chances, she forced a polite smile of her own and perched on the edge of the leather club chair.

Haskel leaned closer, and his expensive cologne clogged her nostrils, making her stifle a sneeze. ''What are you, Miss Quinlan? A model? A movie star?''

Even for a consummate politician, Haskel was laying it on thick, but, remembering the purpose of her father's visit, Laura tolerated the man's line of bull and tried to appear flattered.

"I'm director of public relations at the Quinlan Research Institute," she explained with more civility than she felt. "I enjoy working with my father."

"And well you should." Haskel shook her father's hand and waved Josiah into the seat beside her. "He's the foremost scientist in biological weapons research."

Her father leaned forward in his chair. "Thank you for meeting with us today, Harry. We're at a breakthrough point at the lab, and it's imperative we have more funding."

"You don't beat around the bush, do you, Josiah?" The governor's smile was warm but only touched the surface. Laura wondered what unknown depths his affable veneer concealed.

"I don't want to waste your time," Josiah said. "I know you're a busy man."

Harry rubbed his hands together. "Then let's get to it." He hesitated and glanced toward Laura. "Uh, this your first visit to the capitol, Miss Quinlan?"

Laura blinked at the sudden shift in conversation. "Yes, it is."

Harry reached down, gripped her elbow and lifted her from her seat. "Then why don't you take the tour while your father and I talk? I'm sure you don't want to bother that pretty head with dry financial business."

At the pleading look on her father's face, Laura

bit back a sharp reply. A chauvinistic male like Haskel was oblivious to the fact that Laura knew more about finances than her father, but setting the governor straight wouldn't help their cause. She smiled her brightest smile. "That's a great idea. I'll leave you two to talk."

Struck by a sudden impulse, she bent down and planted a quick kiss on her father's cheek. "I'll be waiting on the front steps when you're finished here."

"I won't be long," her father promised.

"It was a pleasure meeting you, Governor Haskel." She turned and fled the office before the politician could shower her with more patronizing platitudes.

She left the governor's anteroom with a worried frown. Her father was the typical absentminded professor, totally absorbed in his work. Without her reminders, he wouldn't rest, would forget to eat and probably rarely change his clothes. She hoped he would remember now to refer to the request they'd worked up together for more state grant money. He also needed to persuade the governor to use his influence with ranking members of his party in Congress to cough up more federal funds. Josiah's research team was on the brink of a breakthrough, a safe vaccine against a particularly virulent and nasty biological weapon, but they'd need money to push the project to completion.

With a shake of her head, she shrugged off her concerns. Her father's passion for his work spoke for itself. If the governor didn't respond to that, nothing else Josiah could say would convince the man. She checked her watch. In the meantime, she had about a half hour to kill before meeting her father for the drive back to Livingston and the nearby research center.

Haskel had suggested she tour the capitol building, but neither architecture nor government had ever been one of Laura's interests. She was much more fascinated by people. Finding a comfortable chair in an alcove where two main hallways intersected, she settled in to engage in people watching, one of her favorite pastimes.

The first person to pass by was a young woman in a FedEx uniform, who sprinted past with a package and an electronic clipboard tucked beneath her arm. Another woman, clutching a stack of overflowing file folders, tottered by in too-high heels. Following close behind the secretary, two men, apparently legislators, argued loudly over an upcoming increase in the gasoline tax.

A billowing noise floated up the hallway like the chattering of dozens of tiny birds. Laura glanced to her left to see a beleaguered teacher leading a line of children toward her. The students, who looked about first-grade age, walked in pairs, hand in hand.

Laura's heart melted at the sight. She adored children. Just five years ago, she'd wanted children of her own more than anything. A blond-headed boy and girl with big blue eyes, just like their father, babies to cuddle and love. While most of her friends avidly pursued high-powered careers, she had wanted nothing more than to stay home and bake cookies,

welcome her children when they returned home from
school, drive them to soccer games, help with their
homework and attend PTA meetings. She had wanted
to be a mother. Her career could wait until the nest
was empty.

But Curt, blast his cheating heart, had smashed her
dreams of motherhood—and marriage. He had
played the ardent husband so skillfully, his affair
with his old college flame had caught her completely
by surprise. And worst of all, when she'd confronted
him, he'd shown no remorse. Her faith in men shattered, she had filed for divorce. After that, she had
devoted herself to her father and his work, the two
things in life she knew would never let her down.

With a longing heart, she watched the children
pass in front of her, many waving with shy smiles
and giggles. She waggled her fingers at them. But
their smiles suddenly vanished when an alarm blared
through the halls. Several clapped their hands over
their ears to block out the screeching signal. At the
head of the line, the teacher stopped, panic in her
eyes, and took a quick head count.

"What's that noise, Miss Walker?" a small boy
near the front of the line asked.

Before the teacher could answer, a member of the
capitol police force rounded the corner and announced in a booming voice, "It's just a routine fire
drill, folks. Please proceed to the nearest exit as
quickly as possible and keep moving away from the
building."

He continued at a run down the hallway. Laura
pushed to her feet and thought immediately of her

father, then dismissed her concern. Josiah was in the governor's office, probably the first place the police would evacuate in case of trouble.

The teacher completed her count and whipped her head from side to side, craning up and down the hall.

Laura approached the troubled woman. "Something wrong?"

Miss Walker's eyes were wide with fear. "I'm three students short. My aide's taken a sick child to the bus, and I can't leave the rest of the class to look for the missing ones."

Laura patted her arm. "Take your class outside. I'll find the other students and bring them to you."

The teacher practically wilted with relief before anxiety filled her eyes again. "It *is* just a drill, isn't it?"

"That's what the man said," Laura assured her, but she'd seen the sweat on the policeman's forehead and the tight white line around his lips. Something was up.

Miss Walker clapped her hands. "Let's do what the nice policeman said, class. Just like a fire drill at school. Follow me, and *no* talking."

The teacher and her class headed toward the exit. Laura turned the opposite way to retrace their steps, hoping to find the stragglers quickly and shoo them out of the building behind their teacher.

No such luck.

She sprinted down corridor upon corridor in the warren of offices, moving against the tide of evacuees, but found no sign of the missing children. She had almost decided to abandon this portion of the capitol and move to another area when she heard a young boy's shrill voice.

"I know you're in there. You can't fool me."

She raced around the corner to find a little boy with shaggy brown hair standing with his hands on his hips in front of a door that read Women.

"Come out of there right now, Jennifer and Tiffany. Miss Walker's gonna be mad."

Giggles sounded behind the rest-room door. "You can't come in here, Jeremy. This is for girls only."

"Need some help?" Laura asked Jeremy.

He nodded solemnly. "Miss Walker's gonna be mad, but they won't come out."

Laura walked to the rest-room door and pushed it wide. Two little girls with impish grins hovered just beyond the threshold. "You hear that noise?" Laura asked.

Their grins dissolved. Both nodded.

"That's a fire alarm. It means we have to leave the building."

"*Told* you," Jeremy taunted his classmates behind her back.

"Miss Walker has already taken the rest of the class outside. Everyone else in the building has left. You'd better come with me."

The girl with a halo of red hair and a rash of freckles folded her arms across her chest and shook her head. "No way. My mama says I can't go anywhere with strangers."

"You dumbheads!" Jeremy screamed. "C'mon. It's a fire drill."

"You have to go," Laura said calmly. "The police have ordered everyone out of the building. Once we're outside, we'll find Miss Walker and the rest of your class.''

The second girl, her blond hair plaited in a long pigtail, looked at her companion dubiously. "Maybe we better do what she says, Tiffany.''

"Un-uh. Mama says bad people always make up stories to get you to come with them.''

Jennifer glanced up at Laura, then back to her friend. "But that *is* the fire alarm.''

"I won't touch you," Laura pleaded. Her heart pounded, remembering the apprehensive look on the policeman's face. She hadn't smelled smoke. Not yet. But something was wrong, and she had to get these children to safety. "Just follow me out of the building. When you see Miss Walker, you can run to her.''

"Well—''

She could tell Tiffany was wavering. "Come on, hurry now. We don't have much time.''

Tiffany looked to Jennifer, who nodded her consent. In the hallway, Jeremy hopped from one boot to the other. "Hurry up, you dumb girls.''

Laura motioned the girls past her. Just as they crossed the threshold, the floor heaved beneath them, throwing them off their feet.

A concussive blast pierced Laura's ears.

The world around her turned black.

"FOUR MINUTES to the capitol," Frank announced over the chopper's intercom. The suburbs of Helena were visible below them through the helicopter's Plexiglas bubble.

Kyle sank back in his seat and willed his tensed muscles to relax. It looked as if he would have a shot at that bomb after all. He focused his concentration on the details the Helena bomb squad had provided about the device, keeping his mind on the intricacies of its construction, the sequence of contacts to disconnect, the possible permutations of design that could trap the unsuspecting.

With bombs, he was in his element, for the first time since coming to Montana. Not that he wasn't an outdoorsman. He'd grown up on his parents' farm in southern California, working the citrus groves that provided their livelihood. But when he'd arrived at the Lonesome Pony last month, he hadn't known a damn thing about ranches or horses. Hadn't known an Appaloosa from a lalapalooza. Had never settled his butt in a saddle, much less spent the day in one. He'd had to work hard to master enough knowledge to pull his share of the load, but Daniel and Court had been good teachers—

A strong current buffeted the chopper, interrupting his thoughts.

"What the hell was that?" Frank fought to maintain control of the whirlybird.

"God help us!" Court's awe-filled prayer echoed through his headset, and he pointed straight ahead.

Kyle leaned forward between the two front seats for a better view, and his heart stuttered at the sight. A cloud of smoke and dust rose from Helena, precisely over the spot where the capitol building stood.

"Damn," Kyle swore. "If we'd moved a few minutes faster, I might have prevented that."

Court turned in his seat to face Kyle. "Or been blown up with the rest of the building."

Kyle shuddered at that possibility and glanced back over at Daniel. "I'm sorry. We're too late."

The older man's face had gone pale beneath its weathered tan, and he seemed to fight to regain his composure. "Not too late to help. Frank, put us down as close as you can. We have to make sure everyone's out of there."

Like the pro he was, Frank set the helicopter down smoothly on a swath of capitol parking lot that had evidently been cleared before the explosion. One side of the building was in ruins, office walls blown away, furniture hanging from the floors slanting at precarious angles. In stark contrast to the devastation, the other side of the building appeared unscathed. Police cars, fire trucks and ambulances, sirens wailing, were converging on the scene. In a far corner of the lot, paramedics were setting up a triage station.

Kyle was first off the chopper. The stench of cordite and burning electrical wires filled his nose, and plaster dust choked his lungs. Despite the clamor of emergency sirens, he could hear the shouts and screams of onlookers. A quick survey of the area revealed shock and disbelief on everyone's faces.

Roger Jordan, head of the Bureau of Alcohol, Tobacco and Firearms' Helena office, strode across the debris-littered pavement toward Kyle.

"Everyone out?" Kyle asked.

Jordan shook his head. "We've got a hysterical

teacher over there.'' He wagged his head toward the
capitol mall. "Claims she lost three kids inside.
Some woman volunteered to look for them before
the blast. They didn't make it out.''

Daniel approached. "The governor?''

Jordan set his mouth in a grim line. "Haskel and
his secretary are unaccounted for.''

Daniel turned to his agents. "Looks like our
work's cut out for us. Let's find those folks.''

"We've got extra hard hats with headlamps at our
command post.'' Jordan jerked his thumb behind
him. "You're welcome to them.''

Kyle and his fellow agents followed the ATF
leader and soon were fitted with headgear and addi-
tional flashlights.

"Tread carefully in there,'' Daniel warned them.
"What's left of the building is unstable. I don't want
to lose any of you.''

With grim determination, the agents headed toward the devastated section of the building. Dust and
smoke still billowed and swirled. Firefighters sprayed
high-pressure hoses where flames continued to rage.
Taking a deep breath, Kyle stepped into the ruins.

It was like plunging into hell.

LAURA STRUGGLED to her feet, coughing and chok-
ing on dust and smoke. Her first thoughts were of
her father, and she prayed he had been safely evacuated with the governor. Her head throbbed, and although her ears rang from the concussion of the blast,
she could hear the children crying around her. Her

eyes ran so thick with tears, she couldn't see the youngsters in the dim light.

Dear God, if she was this scared, how terrified were they?

"Kids?" she called. "Where are you? Are you all right?"

A pair of tiny arms snaked around her hips. "I'm scared. I want out of here."

It was Tiffany's voice. Laura stooped down and hugged the child. "Hear those sirens? The firefighters are coming. They'll get us out."

A scrambling noise sounded in the wreckage beside her. "Jennifer?"

The other little girl, her body racked with sobs, threw herself at Laura. "I wanna go home. I want my mommy!"

Laura gathered Jennifer against her side. "It's going to be okay, sweetheart. Jeremy, are you out there?"

A low moan answered her call. It seemed to come from a few feet in front of her.

"Hold on to my skirt, girls, and stick together. We have to find Jeremy."

Falling to her hands and knees, Laura crawled toward the sound of the moaning with the two girls close beside her. Debris scraped her knees and tore at her stockings, and she was operating almost blind in the suffocating dust. "I'm coming, Jeremy. Hang on."

Her outstretched hand touched a boot, and she quickly lifted the little boy in her arms. "I've got you now. You'll be okay soon."

With Jennifer and Tiffany clinging to her for dear life, she headed back the way they'd come until she felt a solid wall ahead of her. She turned, braced her back against the wall as she sat, and settled Jeremy on her lap. The dust was beginning to settle, and she could make out the outlines of his stark white face.

And the nasty, bleeding gash across his forehead.

Wriggling out of her suit jacket, she took off her white silk blouse and tore a strip off the bottom. She tore a second strip, folded it into a pad and placed it against the gash on Jeremy's head.

"Be a brave boy," she murmured to him as she pressed the pad against the wound and tied it firmly with the other strip. "This may hurt."

Jeremy only whimpered, and she prayed he didn't have more serious internal injuries. She held him in her arms, crooning reassurances to him, and the girls huddled on either side of her. "We're going to be all right. They'll come for us soon."

As the dust settled, she began to comprehend their situation. The explosion—a gas main, perhaps?—had trapped them in the short access corridor to the ladies' room. The framing of that alcove must have protected them from falling beams and debris, but their approach to the main hall was blocked. There was a hole large enough to lift the children through, but she had no idea what pitfalls lay on the other side. She didn't dare send them out alone, and she feared the whole structure might tumble if she tried to clear her way out.

She could still smell smoke, but she could also hear the sirens of the fire engines, the distant shouts of firefighters, and the splash of water from their hoses. If Miss Walker and the rest of her class had escaped the building, the teacher would have alerted the authorities that Laura and the children were still trapped inside.

The only thing to do was wait.

And keep the children calm.

Jeremy lay still in her arms, but his pulse was steady and his breathing even. Jennifer and Tiffany sniffled on either side of her, and her hearts went out to the terrified little girls. She'd be crying herself, but she had to keep up a brave front for the children.

"Miss Walker knows we're in here," she reassured the girls, "and she'll have the firefighters looking for us. We'll have to make some noise to lead them to us."

Tiffany wiped her nose on her sleeve. "I can scream real loud."

"Screaming isn't a good idea," Laura suggested with more calm than she felt. "We don't want to frighten anyone." *Or get you more worked up than you already are.* "How about a song we could all sing?"

Jennifer gazed up at her through soot-rimmed eyes. "I know 'This Old Man.'"

"Me, too," Tiffany said.

"Good," Laura said.

In the far distance, blending with the noises of sirens, she could hear people moving through the ruins, shouting to one another. "If we sing real loud, the firefighters will hear us and come find us. Ready?"

Their voices were raspy and thin as they began to sing, and little Jeremy lay entirely too quietly in her arms. But as the singing cleared the dust from their throats, their song grew louder and more steady. They continued gamely, verse after verse.

"'This Old Man, he played eight—'"

"Hello! Where are you?"

Laura and the girls broke off midphrase at the call. The voice that hailed them was rich and deep and coming from where the main hall had been before the blast.

"We're in here," Laura called.

She heard the sounds of debris shifting and someone approaching. A beam of light shone through the small opening that led to the main hall.

Laura blinked in the glare and felt Tiffany and Jennifer cling tighter to her.

The light beam withdrew, and another light, more powerful and widespread than the flashlight, filled the crevice. A big man with wide shoulders thrust his head through the small opening.

Laura caught her breath. He looked like an avenging angel with a hard hat for a halo. Even with smoke and dust smearing his face, she could discern the strong lines of his jaw, the classic slope of his nose and the intense green eyes that glowed with compassion and concern. His expression radiated kindness and a virile gentleness, and she realized with a jolt that there was resolution and incredible strength there as well. His smile melted the icy knot of fear in her stomach and hope surged in its place.

"Don't worry," he said casually, as if they'd met in an elevator instead of a bombed-out building. "I'm Kyle Foster, and my friends and I will have you out of here in no time."

Chapter Two

"You're an answer to a prayer," Laura tried to shout, but her voice was hoarse from dust and singing.

Her rescuer's mouth curved in a slow, sensuous smile that would have weakened her knees—if she'd had any strength left and hadn't been already sitting. She hoped he was as courageous as he appeared. He'd promised to get them out, but she could hear the building falling around them. Only someone with nerves of steel would risk being buried alive to help people he didn't know.

"Just keep those prayers coming till we're out of here," he called in a deep, resonant voice filled with steady reassurance.

Jeremy stirred in Laura's arms, and her anxiety for the child increased. "I have a little boy who's hurt," she called.

Kyle's smile disappeared, and concern filled his eyes. "How bad?"

"Don't know," Laura replied out of honesty and a reluctance to frighten Tiffany and Jennifer any more than they already were.

"Can you bring him to me?" Kyle said with a calmness that eased her racing heart. "We'll take him out first."

Laura struggled to her feet with the boy in her arms. "Stay here, girls. I'll be back for you."

She picked her way carefully through the wreckage toward the opening to the main corridor. Stumbling once, she almost fell, and chunks of plaster rained down on her. She hunched over Jeremy to shield him with her body and struggled to maintain her balance in that awkward pose.

The boy roused again and looked up at her through unfocused eyes. "Mommy?"

"No, sweetheart, I'm Laura."

She thought of his mother, of the parents of all three children and how frantic they must be to have their youngsters out of danger and back in their arms.

And she thought of her own father, waiting outside for her rescue, desperate to see her unharmed.

Soon, Daddy, she promised. *Don't worry about me.*

"You're almost here." Kyle's encouraging voice echoed through the wreckage. "Keep coming."

"My arm hurts," Jeremy whimpered.

She bit back tears at the little boy's pain. "We'll have you fixed up real soon."

When she reached the opening, Kyle was gone, and she panicked, wondering if they'd been deserted. Debris continued to fall in the stillness of the wreckage, and she feared the rest of the building might collapse any moment.

"Hello? Anyone there?" she called.

Kyle's handsome face reappeared, and she chastised herself for her lack of faith in him. She should have known from the reliable look in his amazing green eyes that the man wouldn't desert them.

"I've sent my partner after the paramedics and a stretcher." He couldn't fit his wide shoulders through the narrow hole, but he thrust his arms, clad in a denim jacket, into the opening. She noted the strong, slender fingers and square nails, streaked with dirt and marred with nicks and scratches from clawing through the wreckage.

"Let me have him," Kyle said. "We'll take good care of him."

"Careful," Laura warned as she transferred Jeremy. "His arm may be broken."

With a gentleness she hadn't expected in such a rugged man, Kyle took the boy in his arms as carefully as if the child were made of glass. A tear slid down the man's face, but Laura couldn't tell if he cried for the child or if the dust from the wreckage irritated his eyes.

Jeremy opened his eyes and gazed up at Kyle. "Who are you?"

"I'm helping the firefighters, big guy." The man's voice was kind and encouraging. "My friends and I will get you out of here and find your mother."

Jeremy relaxed in his arms. Kyle maneuvered the boy's body through the narrow aperture, and the two disappeared.

"I'll be back for the rest of you," Laura heard Kyle call.

She returned to Jennifer and Tiffany, grabbed each

one by a hand and helped them pick their way through the tangle of beams, wires and drywall to the opening, their only route of escape.

"Will he come back?" Jennifer asked, once again sniffling with fear.

"He'll be back." Laura placed a supportive arm around the girl's shoulders. She didn't have to fake confidence. Something about the man, the assurance in his eyes, the tenor of his voice, told her Kyle Foster was a man who didn't make empty promises.

A horrific boom reverberated behind them in the rest room, and a major portion of the ceiling gave way and crashed to the floor. The girls screamed, and Laura jumped. If they'd stayed where they'd been earlier, all of them would have been crushed. What remained of the building was deteriorating fast, and if Kyle didn't return soon, they might be buried alive.

She pulled the girls close to bolster their courage and tried to squelch her own rising panic. "He'll be here any minute now."

True to his word, Kyle thrust his face through the opening. Laura had never been so glad to see anyone in her life. How could any man look so damn sexy with so much dirt on him and seem so at ease with a building raining down around his ears?

"Who's next?" he asked.

Laura felt Tiffany stiffen against her. "You go, Jennifer," the little redhead insisted. "I'm older. I'll stay here and look after the lady."

"You're not older." Jennifer sniffed. "We're both six."

"I'm six and a half," Tiffany said in a superior tone.

"You're both coming," Kyle said. "I have people with me to carry you out."

The urgency in the look he threw Laura set her into instant motion. She scooped Jennifer into her arms and handed her to Kyle. He threaded the girl through the opening as if she weighed no more than the dust that swirled around them, a testament to the strength in the well-developed muscles of his arms.

"What's a good-looking kid like you doing in a mess like this?" he asked Jennifer. She responded to his teasing grin by throwing her arms around his neck and holding tight.

With a tenderness that brought tears to Laura's eyes, Kyle patted the girl's back, then handed her off to someone behind him. He immediately shoved his arms through the opening again. "Next?"

Laura picked up Tiffany. The girl leaned back in her arms and looked at her. "Aren't you coming?"

"In a minute," Laura said.

"But the hole's too small." Tiffany locked gazes with her, eyes filled with worry, as Kyle took the girl from Laura's arms. "How will you get out?"

"Don't worry." Kyle spoke to Tiffany but his eyes met Laura's. "We won't leave your friend in there."

He disappeared for a moment. When he returned, he thrust a hard hat and his own denim jacket through the hole toward Laura. "Put these on and move as far from the opening as you can. We're going to frame some supports before we tear open this hole."

Only then did Laura realize she'd been standing there the whole time in only her bra and skirt. She'd thrown aside her jacket, now buried beneath the wreckage behind her, and used her blouse to bind Jeremy's wounds. But Kyle Foster had acted as if finding a woman only half dressed in the halls of the capitol building was nothing out of the ordinary.

She tugged on his jacket, still warm from his body heat, and was inundated with a melange of scents: sunshine, meadow grasses, saddle soap, leather and a pleasingly masculine musk. As she slid her arms into the sleeves, it was as if Kyle Foster had wrapped his arms around her, a comfortable illusion. The thought and the jacket warmed her. She hadn't realized how hard she'd been shivering until she stopped. Caring for the children, she hadn't had time to think about herself. Now, the solitude and vulnerability of her situation hit her full force.

Her distress must have shown in her eyes, because Kyle reached out through the opening, his eyes fierce with emotion, his jaw set with determination, his lips curved in an encouraging smile, and ran his fingers down her cheek in a tender salute. "You're a hell of a brave lady."

She didn't want to move, to break the warm, heartening contact of his touch. She wanted to lean into the cup of his hand, the only place in this hellhole of a building she felt safe.

He patted her cheek and gently shoved her away. "Move. Now," he ordered.

Jamming the hard hat on, she scurried back against the wall of the access corridor.

"Don't be alarmed," Kyle spoke through the opening. "You'll hear a lot of noise out here, chain saws and jackhammers. We have to clear a path for you. There'll be some debris shaken loose. Hunch down against the wall and keep that hard hat on."

"I understand."

"Hey." He took off his own hard hat and thrust his head through the opening. His forehead was tanned above the line of plaster dust and his hair a golden brown, a perfect complement to his eyes, the deep green of summer leaves. "You're going to be fine. I'll get you out."

This time he didn't smile, but there was intensity and solemn promise in his expression.

His confidence was infectious. She nodded and huddled closer to the wall.

He broke into a grin then, an appealing expression that made her wish she'd met this man before in another time and place.

"Better stick your fingers in your ears— Sorry, I don't know your name."

"Laura, Laura Quinlan."

"Stop up your ears, Laura. The noise will be brutal."

He pulled back and was gone. True to his word, the scream of chain saws and thunder of jackhammers assaulted her senses and sent a rain of dust and debris around her. She crouched low and raised her arms above her head, praying her rescuers would reach her before the building collapsed on top of her. The bone-jolting racket seemed to go on forever.

Then, suddenly, it was quiet.

Before she could lift her head, she felt someone grip her elbows and lift her to her feet. She glanced up into Kyle Foster's grimy but handsome face.

"C'mon, Laura." His face lit with the same killer smile. "We're busting out of this joint."

Before she could protest, he swept her off her feet and into his arms.

"I can walk," she protested.

He gripped her tighter. "You don't know the way through the wreckage."

In spite of carrying her, he moved with a swiftness that amazed her, surefooted on the treacherous debris. She twined her arms around his neck and held on tight, her face buried against the broad expanse of his chest.

Dust clouds choked them.

Debris tumbled around them.

Although her rescuer seemed calm, she could feel his urgency in the fierce pounding of his heart beneath her cheek. Her own heartbeat thundered in her ears. What if the building collapsed on top of them?

Suddenly she was blinded by daylight.

Laura heard cheers go up from a group of people in the distance. She lifted her head and saw a band of firefighters, police officers and paramedics gathered in the parking lot, applauding and smiling.

"You can set me down now," she told Kyle. She preferred to face the crowd of strangers on her own two feet.

"Nope. Not until the paramedics check you out."

A thundering roar and a blast of dust hit them from behind, and Kyle staggered slightly, still heading for the group in the parking lot. The waiting crowd went silent.

"My God!" Laura said. "What was that?"

"The building." Kyle's rich voice was tight with emotion. "The ruins caved in. We got you out just in time."

"The children?"

"Everybody's out. We were the last ones."

She sagged against him in relief.

Ahead of them, the crowd parted, forming a corridor to the triage center the paramedics had set up. Kyle slid her onto a chair beneath the awning strung from the back of the truck. A young woman in paramedic blues took Laura's blood pressure, checked her pulse, listened to her heart and lungs, and did a quick body scan for injuries.

Kyle remained by her side. "She okay?" he asked the medic.

The woman nodded. "But I want her to stay here for now so we can keep an eye on her, just in case."

"The little boy," Laura said, "Jeremy. How is he?"

"Broken arm," the medic replied. "And a concussion. We've already transported him to the hospital. But he should be fine in a few days."

"His parents?"

"They were waiting for him," the medic said. "As soon as the explosion hit the news, we've had the parents of children in that class pouring in here to learn if their kids were safe. Jeremy's parents rode in the ambulance with him."

"And the little girls?" Laura looked around for

Jennifer and Tiffany, but didn't see them. Only then did she notice that Kyle had disappeared.

"They both checked out okay," the paramedic said. "Their parents took them home. Wanted them away from all this as soon as possible."

Laura glanced behind her at the awful wreckage and shuddered. "Can't say that I blame them."

Kyle Foster reappeared and handed her a bottle of water. "This will clear the dust from your throat."

She accepted it with thanks and drank. Water had never tasted so good. When she'd finished, she remembered she was wearing his jacket. "If the paramedics will loan me a blanket," she said, "I can return your coat."

"Keep it," he said. "You can return it later."

"But it's getting late. And colder."

His slow grin made her pulse race. "I'll be too busy for a while to be cold."

She remembered her father then, dressed only in his best suit. At his age, he chilled easily. She needed to find him quickly and take him away from the destruction that surrounded them, back to the warmth and security of home.

She stood, silently cursing the weakness in her legs. "I have to find my father."

Kyle apparently noticed her unsteadiness. He grasped her elbow and braced her against him.

"You really should stay quiet," the medic warned.

Laura cast a pleading glance at Kyle. "Please, I need to know he's all right."

Kyle nodded. "There's a check-in area for evacuees across the lot. I'll go with you."

"But you have work—"

"This is part of it."

He helped her pick her way through snarls of fire hoses, clusters of emergency vehicles and crowds of panicked people, also searching for their relatives. When Laura and Kyle reached the checkpoint, it was mobbed.

"You don't have to stay," Laura said. "Looks like I'll be standing in line a while."

"Your father wasn't with you in the building?" Kyle asked.

Laura shook her head. "He was meeting with the governor."

The sudden careful stillness on Kyle's face frightened her. "Wait here," he said. "I'll be right back."

He was gone only a couple of minutes before he returned. "Come with me. The governor's in the sheriff's command center."

"And my father?"

Kyle didn't answer. With a protective arm around her shoulders, he threaded them through the teeming, sometimes hysterical crowd to the edge of the lot. He knocked on the door of what looked like a huge recreational vehicle except for the lettering and insignia that clearly marked it as the sheriff's command center.

An officer opened the door and offered his hand to Laura to guide her up the stairs. Kyle followed. Inside, Governor Haskel, a bandage around his head and his arm in a sling, pushed up from his chair and approached her. For once, his smooth, political smile was absent, his charismatic face grimly set.

Laura whipped her head around, searching for her father.

He wasn't there.

"Where's Daddy?" she asked the governor. "Was he hurt? Have they taken him to the hospital?"

Harry Haskel shook his head. "I'm sorry, Laura. Your father…he was killed in the blast."

"What?" Everything took on a surreal aspect. She saw everything through a muted haze. The handsome, sympathetic face of Kyle Foster, whose strong arms kept her from falling. The silent sheriff's deputies who manned their posts without looking at her. The pained expression of the governor.

"There must be some mistake," she pleaded in desperation. "Have you checked the hospitals?"

The governor's expression didn't change, and when he spoke, his usually booming, hale-and-hearty voice was gentle. "I'm sorry, Laura. We've confirmed it. Your father's dead."

The last thing she remembered was Kyle Foster catching her as she fell.

KYLE STOPPED the night-duty nurse as she came out of Laura's hospital room. "May I see her now?"

The stout woman nodded, but fixed him with a stern stare. "Don't stay long. She's had a terrible shock and needs her rest."

Kyle hesitated before entering, wondering if he was doing the right thing. At the hotel, where he and the other agents had showered and changed after long hours of investigation and conferring with the other authorities, he had debated whether to visit Laura or not. He knew she was grieving, that she probably wanted her privacy, but he couldn't get her out of his mind.

In the bombed-out building that afternoon, he'd heard her long before he'd met her. He'd caught the clear, pure notes of her soprano voice leading the children in song, guiding the rescuers to them. And when he'd seen her, her long dark hair framing her pale face like a midnight cloud, her startling blue eyes calm and bright, he'd been amazed by her composure. She'd stripped away her blouse to bandage the boy's wound, but she'd exhibited no false modesty. In fact, she'd been so centered on keeping the children calm, he would swear she'd been totally unaware how provocatively gorgeous she'd looked, clad only in a short skirt that emphasized her slender hips and revealed slim legs, and a wispy piece of lace that did little to hide her small, firm breasts.

She'd been an angel to those children. Without her assistance, he doubted he and the others could have moved them from the building as quickly.

And after all her bravery and help, she'd lost her father.

Damn. Life wasn't fair.

Encountering no one else in the waiting room and observing no one except the nurses coming and going from Laura's room, he decided she needed a friend. Taking a deep breath and warning himself not to screw things up and upset her even more, he stepped into the room.

She lay propped against pillows as white as her flawless complexion, eyes closed, with long lashes lying dusky against her cheeks. Someone had brushed the dust from her luxuriant hair, spread like a dark halo on the pillow. And someone had washed the grime from her lovely face, its only shortcoming now the paleness in her cheeks. He'd touched the soft silkiness of her cheek in the corridor of the ruined building, and he was consumed now with a desire to touch her again.

He moved beside the bed, and she opened her eyes.

"I came by to check on you." He silently cursed himself for his awkwardness. She needed comforting, but he couldn't find the words.

She curved her lips slightly in a smile of recognition. "I'm not very lucid. I think they've pumped me full of tranquilizers."

"You've had a terrible shock. I'm sorry about your father."

Tears welled in her magnificent blue eyes. "My mother died when I was born. I don't have brothers or sisters. Daddy's been my entire family...."

He sat on the side of the bed and gathered her long, slender fingers folded atop the coverlet into his own. Her hands were cold, and he rubbed them gently to warm them. "I wish I could help."

She blinked away tears. "You did help. You saved my life. Are you a firefighter?"

He shook his head. "Just happened to be in town. I work at the Lonesome Pony Ranch near Livingston."

Her eyes widened in surprise. "With C.J. and Frank Connolly?"

"That's right. Frank's gone to get C.J. Figured you'd want her here with you."

He'd be glad when C.J. arrived to stay with her. C.J. was one of the top researchers at the Quinlan Research Institute owned by Laura's father. A couple months ago, Frank had saved C.J. from kidnapping by Gilad, a member of the Black Order terrorists anxious to learn what the British scientist knew about biological weapons and how to stop them. Frank had fallen in love with the beautiful researcher and married her.

He remembered C.J. telling him that since assuming her post at the research lab several weeks ago, she had become close friends with Laura Quinlan. Not so close, however, that C.J. had divulged to Laura or anyone else at the facility the true nature of the work at the Lonesome Pony Ranch. As far as the Quinlans and the other scientists were concerned, C.J. had married a cowboy, not an undercover agent.

Laura closed her eyes, and her fingers squeezed his tightly.

Poor kid, he thought, then corrected himself. Not a kid. Laura Quinlan had to be in her late twenties, according to what C.J. had told him.

Laura opened her eyes. "Nobody will talk to me, except to say I'll be all right. Please, tell me what happened to my father."

Kyle swallowed hard. He wasn't about to cause her more anguish by describing the gruesome extent of Josiah Quinlan's injuries. "He died quickly. I doubt he felt anything or even knew what happened."

He could tell from her expression she was in total denial of her father's death, and her next words confirmed his fear. "Everyone else in the building was evacuated. Daddy must have been, too. Maybe he's lost his memory and is wandering the city somewhere. Has anyone looked for him?"

"Laura, the governor was in the same room." Kyle was firm but empathetic. "He identified your father's body."

Yanking her hands from his grasp, she propped herself on her elbows, eyes blazing like blue fire. "Why?"

With patience he'd learned from dealing with his strong-willed daughter, Molly, Kyle grasped her shoulders and gently pressed her back against the pillows. "Promise you'll stay calm, and I'll answer all your questions. Otherwise, Nurse Godzilla will throw me out of here on my ear."

As if all the strength had gone out of her, Laura sagged against the pillows. "Why didn't Daddy and the governor evacuate like everybody else?"

Hers was a good question, one Kyle and the other investigators had pressed the governor about. "Governor Haskel said his secretary came in when the alarm sounded. She told him one of the capitol police had just assured her the alarm was simply a malfunction in the system. That there was no need for the governor to interrupt his business to evacuate."

Groggy with medication, Laura shook her head. "I don't understand."

"Someone wanted to make certain the governor's office wasn't empty when the bomb blew."

"Bomb?" The word seemed to hit her like a blast. "The explosion wasn't an accident?"

Kyle shook his head.

"I didn't know," she murmured. "I thought maybe it was a leak in a natural-gas line…"

For several minutes she remained so still, eyes closed, he thought she'd drifted back to sleep. He started to rise from the side of the bed, but she gripped his hand and opened her eyes. He could see her fighting against confusion and the effects of the drugs she'd been given.

"My father was murdered."

She'd stated a fact, not asked a question, so Kyle said nothing.

"Did the secretary identify the policeman who told them to stay?" she asked.

"Haskel's secretary, your father and a policeman doing a final sweep to clear the building were the only fatalities."

This time she'd didn't contradict him about her father. She was either in shock or finally coming to grips with his death.

She raised her face and fixed her tear-filled, periwinkle-blue gaze on him. "Why…how could the governor survive and not Daddy?"

Another good question. Even in the depths of grief and the haze of tranquilizers, she exhibited a remarkable grasp of what was important.

"According to the governor's account," Kyle explained, "he was leaning down to remove something from the bottom drawer of his desk when the blast occurred. The massive piece of mahogany furniture between him and the direction of the blast absorbed most of the impact.''

Tears overflowed her eyes and trickled down her cheeks. Her full bottom lip quivered. ''And Daddy was on the other side of the desk.''

''I'm sorry.''

She swiped away the tears with the back of her hand. ''Thank you for telling me. I had to know, no matter how awful…''

He marveled at her poise. Even under the most horrific circumstances, she was thoughtful and kind, considerate of others in spite of her grief. If, as she'd said, Josiah Quinlan had raised her on his own, the man had done a damn good job.

He thought of Molly, abandoned by her mother, with only Kyle to take care of her. Molly would be counting on him for everything. He hoped he could do half as good a job as Josiah had with his daughter.

Laura turned her head on the pillow toward the table where he'd emptied his hands when he'd entered the room. Following her gaze, he picked up the bouquet of pink roses he'd left there. ''I'll have the nurse put these in some water.''

''Thank you.'' A ghost of a smile tugged at her lips. ''And the science fiction video game?''

''For Jeremy. He's in the pediatric wing on the next floor. I thought I'd check on him before heading back to the ranch.''

''You are a remarkable man, Kyle.''

Embarrassed by her praise, he shook his head.

''Please, one more question?'' she asked.

He nodded.

"Why am I here? I don't have any injuries, do I?"

"No physical injuries, but you've suffered severe emotional trauma. They're just keeping you for observation." He didn't add how Daniel Austin had pulled strings to have her admitted, to make sure she had someone to watch out for her until C.J. arrived. Laura had no relatives, and Daniel had made certain she wasn't left alone to deal with her father's death. "You'll be released in the morning, and C.J. can take you home."

He heard footsteps and glanced into the hallway to see Frank and C.J. waiting outside the door. "I have to go."

Laura still reminded him of an angel—a grief-stricken angel. "You've been very kind," she said.

This time he couldn't resist the impulse to touch her. He cupped the side of her face in his hand. "Get some sleep."

He wished he could assure her that everything would be all right in the morning, but he couldn't. With her father dead, it would be a long time before things would feel all right again for Laura Quinlan.

She leaned against his hand and closed her eyes. He waited, cradling her face until he was certain she'd fallen asleep. Then he slipped quietly from the room.

Motioning to Frank and C.J., he led them to the visitors' lounge at the end of the corridor, thinking as he always did when he saw them together what a handsome couple they made, Frank with his dark hair and military bearing and C.J. with her honey-blond hair and curvaceous figure—and both with minds as sharp as steel traps.

"How is she?" C.J. asked in her clipped British accent.

"Taking it hard, but she's sleeping now." Kyle glanced at Frank and noted the tension in his expression. "What's happened?"

Frank, his exhaustion showing, ran his hand over his short, military-cut hair. "There was a break-in at the Quinlan Research Institute this afternoon."

"And?" Kyle asked, sensing the worst.

C.J.'s light-brown eyes telegraphed her anxiety. "Someone's stolen enough D-5 to poison every city water system in Montana."

Chapter Three

"Finish your breakfast, doodlebug," Kyle said to Molly. She graced him with an adoring smile, and wonder filled him at how much he could love one tiny human being.

He sat with his daughter in the large, sunny kitchen at the ranch. Daniel and the other agents had eaten earlier, but Kyle had waited to have breakfast with Molly.

He finished the last bite of feather-light pancakes with huckleberry syrup and handed his empty plate to Dale McMurty, the ranch's cook and housekeeper, who also watched Molly while Kyle was working.

"Excellent breakfast, as always, Mrs. Mac."

"Better for eatin' than wearin'." The plump older woman grinned and nodded toward Molly whose face, round with baby fat, was smeared with purple syrup.

"Can you ride wif me and Jewel?" Molly took another bite of the pancake Kyle had cut into bits for her.

Jewel, granddaughter of Dale and Patrick McMurty who helped Daniel run the ranch, was teaching Molly to ride on Ribbons, the new pony Kyle had bought her. If he'd had his druthers, he'd spend the morning teaching Molly to ride. But with the Black Order terrorists still on the loose almost four weeks after the bombing, catching them had to be his priority. With a guilty conscience, he braced himself for her disappointment.

"I can't, sweetheart. Daddy has work to do."

"Wif Frank and Court and Daniel?" Her wide, innocent eyes, green like his own, regarded him with a seriousness too old for her years.

"That's right." Her somberness reproached him harder than tears or a temper tantrum would have. She was too young to look so solemn. He reached across the table and tickled her to make her laugh. "But I'll spend tonight after supper with you. You pick out a favorite book for us to read."

Still giggling, Molly clapped her plump hands and bounced up and down in her booster seat. *"Green Eggs and Ham."*

Kyle suppressed a groan. He knew that book by heart, had read it till its singsong nonsense rhymes made him cross-eyed, but it was Molly's favorite, and if she wanted to hear it for the umpteenth time, he'd read it again for his favorite girl.

The back door swung open with a bang, and twelve-year-old Jewel McMurty stomped into the kitchen, blond ponytail swinging. "You ready, shrimp?" she called to Molly. "I got the horses saddled."

"Morning, Jewel." Kyle said. "Molly will be with you in a minute."

He cleaned his daughter's face with a damp paper towel, then helped her into her jacket. "All set?"

Molly jumped up and down with excitement. "I like riding Ribbons."

"Give Daddy a kiss."

She threw her chubby arms around his neck, then hurried toward Jewel who waited at the back door.

"Jewel!" Dale called before her granddaughter could slip out.

"Yes'm?" the girl answered, shifting from one booted foot to the other in her eagerness to get away.

"Is your grandpa out there where he can watch you?"

Jewel nodded. "He's working in the barn."

"You keep a good eye on that young'un, you hear?" Dale stood with her fists on her wide hips, narrowed eyes blazing. "Anything happens to that child, I'll skin you alive and tack your hide next to that Navajo blanket on the lobby wall."

"Yes, ma'am."

"And Jewel?" her grandmother added, her features melting into a loving smile that belied the fierceness of her earlier words. "Take care of yourself while you're at it, girl."

Jewel nodded, grabbed Molly by the hand, whirled on her heel, and the two disappeared before Dale could say another word.

"Young'uns." Dale refilled Kyle's coffee cup. "They're a blessing and a worry."

Kyle watched the two girls cross the yard toward the barn, Molly scuffling her feet in the fine gravel of the driveway. Although Molly's welfare was al-

ways foremost in his thoughts, he had no worries
about leaving her with Jewel McMurty. The twelve-
year-old was a dynamo of energy and gabbiness
packed in her less than five-foot frame, but she was
also levelheaded and dependable. Molly was in good
hands.

He glanced at his watch. Fifteen minutes until he
met with the others in the secret room below the
main house that served as headquarters for Montana
Confidential. He sipped Dale's hot coffee and attempted to review his notes, but a single image kept
intruding on his thoughts.

Laura Quinlan standing in the misting rain at her
father's funeral.

She hadn't known Kyle was there, hadn't known
he was watching. Three days after the bombing, security had been tight at the cemetery. Governor Haskel, still wearing bandages on his injuries, had attended, and since the terrorists had apparently tried
to kill him once, the worry was that they might strike
again.

Kyle and Court had watched the funeral from a
surveillance van with darkened windows, parked a
dozen yards from the gravesite. Using a special telephoto lens, Kyle had snapped shot after shot of every
person who'd attended, but his attention had been
riveted on Laura.

Tragically beautiful, she had stood straight and tall
by her father's flower-draped casket. Elegant in a
trim black coat, black stockings and shoes, she listened to the priest's every word without shedding a
tear. But Kyle could tell from the close-up the lens

gave him that she was all cried out, that she had
already shed more tears than any person should have
to in a lifetime. Her dark blue eyes glistened with
grief, and her generous mouth was firmly set, as if
she'd vowed no more sobs would pass her lips.

The cold, misting rain had etched her cheeks with
color, but her flawless face was otherwise pale and
drawn. Frank and C.J. stood on either side of her,
and several couples, later identified as scientists from
the lab and their spouses, gathered around her, but
Kyle couldn't help remembering her claim in the
hospital that she was all alone.

Numerous times since then, he'd wanted to drive
to the Quinlan laboratory and call on her, to let her
know she had a friend, but he hadn't allowed himself
that pleasure. He'd been too busy with the investigation of the Black Order, and even if he hadn't, he
had to be careful where he was seen and how, in the
event he had to assume an undercover role in the
case.

But he couldn't get his mind off Laura Quinlan
and the bravery she'd shown in helping to save those
children. An extraordinary woman—

He blinked in surprise at where his thoughts had
taken him. Ever since Alicia had deserted him and
Molly over a year ago for her wealthy Hollywood
producer, he'd found his trust in women shattered
and his interest in them gone. Even the most gorgeous, as C.J. definitely was, had held no attraction
for him. But Laura was different. When the Black
Order terrorists were captured and placed behind

bars, he definitely wanted to get to know Laura Quinlan better.

"Kyle?" Whitney MacNair's melodic voice shattered his daydreams.

He glanced up to find Daniel's executive assistant, clipboard in hand, standing in the doorway that led to the hall. Unlike everyone else on the ranch who wore jeans as their standard uniform, Whitney definitely dressed to a different drummer. This morning she wore a long, camel-colored wool skirt and an ecru silk blouse, topped by a dark chocolate velvet vest embroidered in a colorful paisley design. Instead of cowboy boots, she sported calf-hugging high-heeled boots of soft Italian leather. On anyone else, the outfit would have looked out of place, but it complemented Whitney's red-gold hair, gray eyes and peaches-and-cream complexion.

"Morning, Whitney. What's up?"

"Daniel's ready to start the meeting."

Had Kyle really spent the entire fifteen minutes thinking of Laura Quinlan? Flustered, he grabbed his notes and followed in the wake of Whitney's expensive perfume to the secret room below Daniel's study.

The rest of the team was waiting, gathered around the sturdy oak conference table in the middle of their operations center. Kyle took a chair opposite Daniel at the other end of the table, and Whitney slid into an empty seat beside her boss, ready to take notes.

Daniel motioned to Kyle. "Since you're our bomb expert and the one with the chemistry degrees, how about bringing us up to speed?"

Kyle nodded. "Our investigation is two-pronged. Let's deal with the capitol bombing first. ATF analysis of the bomb shows it's definitely Black Order. Its specific signature is identical to bombs the Order claimed credit for in London and Athens two years ago."

Court shook his head. "Joshua Neely failed, but obviously the Black Order had a backup plan."

Tension crackled around the table. All remembered Court's undercover mission with the Sons and Daughters of Montana militia group. The agents had had Neely, the militia leader, under surveillance. Maybe if they'd been able to track down Neely's men who'd blown Court's cover and stolen the explosives, they would have led the agents to the Black Order and its disastrous plot.

"So now we definitely know who," Frank said, "the Black Order, but do we know why?"

Kyle shook his head. "The bombing was possibly a diversion from the Quinlan lab robbery, but the two sites are so far apart, that motive seems a bit of a stretch. From the placement of the bomb and the deliberate attempt to keep the governor in his office, we can assume Harry Haskel was the target."

"Not Josiah Quinlan?" Daniel asked.

Kyle shook his head. "If Quinlan had been the target, he'd have been easier to take out at the Institute. From what the governor told me, Quinlan's appointment was scheduled at the last minute. The terrorists couldn't have known Quinlan would be in the capitol."

"Now we're back to *why* again," Court said.

Whitney cleared her throat and looked to Daniel for permission to speak.

"If you can shed any light on this mess," he said, "be my guest."

"A few months before the bombing," Whitney said, "I set up a dinner party for Senator Ross Weston when he and Haskel had just returned from a trip to the Emirate of Agar. Hasn't that Middle Eastern country been identified as the home base for the Black Order?"

Kyle smiled. Months ago, Whitney, who had worked for Senator Weston, had been the subject of a scandal after the press got hold of reports that Ross had been plying his beautiful and flirtatious assistant with gifts. Horrified, the MacNairs, her very proper, very upper-class and highly influential parents, had temporarily banished Whitney to Daniel's care at the isolated ranch until the press brouhaha blew over. Whitney, however, had managed to keep informed on Washington events.

"You're right, Whitney," Kyle said. "Agar is their base. But are you suggesting Haskel is in collusion with the terrorists?"

Court shook his head. "Doesn't make sense. If he is, why kill him? More likely he and Weston stumbled onto secrets while in Agar that the Order doesn't want them to know. Either that or the Black Order wants to embarrass Weston. After all, he's running for president on an antiterrorist platform."

Kyle nodded. "Looks bad for Weston when terrorists bomb the capitol and almost kill the governor of Weston's home state."

"I'll check with the FBI," Court said, "and see if any threats have been made against Weston."

Daniel appeared thoughtful. "Court's already reported that a joint FBI/ATF raid has captured three of the Order who impersonated capitol police the day of the bombing. But none of the prisoners is talking, which brings our bombing investigation to a stalemate. What about the lab theft, Kyle?"

"The sheriff's office handled the investigation. It appears the intruders rappelled down the canyon wall above the complex, cut the chain-link fence and entered the lab. Once inside, they went straight to storage and took the entire contents of that specific refrigerator. The other test tubes were harmless—sample vaccines, suspension agents—but they did steal enough D-5 to pose a serious threat."

Frank tugged at his ear. "We're waiting for the other shoe to drop. When and where will they use it?"

Court grinned. "At least we've abandoned *why*."

"We know why," Daniel said with a grimace, leaning forward and locking his strong hands together on the gleaming tabletop. "The Order hates the United States. Anything they can do to create chaos and destruction here furthers their goals." He glanced around the table. "Our investigation is deadlocked. We have no leads on the Order's whereabouts, the prisoners aren't talking and the trail is getting colder as we speak. Any suggestions?"

"I have an idea," Kyle said. "From the results of the sheriff's investigation at the Quinlan lab, it appears the Order may have had inside support—"

"God help us," Daniel blurted, and straightened in his chair. "That lab works on vaccines and antidotes for biological warfare, but they also store samples of the biological weapons themselves for testing. If there's an Order member on-site, we've got a much bigger problem than a missing vial of D-5."

Kyle nodded. "That's where my idea comes in. Send me to the lab undercover as a research scientist. With my background in chemistry, not only can I play the part, but I can ferret out any clues that might lead us to the Order's contact at Quinlan's."

Daniel rubbed his chin, thinking. "It might work. But we'd need Laura Quinlan's complete cooperation. She's calling all the shots at the lab now that her father's gone."

"What if she's the one involved with the Order?" Court asked.

"No way," Kyle insisted hotly.

The others stared at him. Frank was nodding in agreement, Court appeared skeptical and Daniel's expression was noncommittal. Whitney, however, was grinning widely, as if she'd just picked up a delicious morsel of D.C. gossip.

Embarrassed by his heated response, Kyle breathed deeply to calm his emotions. "The woman was devastated by her father's death—and almost died herself in that building. She wouldn't have taken part in bombing it."

Frank came to his rescue. "I think Kyle's right. From everything that C.J.'s told me, Laura is devoted to her father's work. The last thing she'd want would be handing over to terrorists the biological weapons her father vowed to stop.''

"We'll have to talk to her before we send Kyle in," Daniel said. "And I tend to agree with Kyle and Frank about her innocence. However—" he raised his head and caught Kyle's gaze along the length of the table "—men have been fooled by beautiful women more times than history can count. Kyle, you'll have to be damn careful under the circumstances, not just to keep from blowing your cover, but to keep yourself alive.''

Daniel's warning threw a definite chill in the air, and Kyle suppressed the urge to shiver. From what he knew of Laura Quinlan, he'd trust her with his life. However, he had to admit there was a lot about her he *didn't* know. And that he was looking forward to finding out.

"It's agreed, then," Daniel said. "Kyle, you'll contact Miss Quinlan—"

"Daniel?" Dale McMurty's raspy voice sounded over the intercom. "Sorry to interrupt, but Kyle's got a visitor. What should I tell 'em?"

"Who is it?" Daniel asked.

"Laura Quinlan. She's waiting in the front room."

"Tell her Kyle will be right there." Daniel looked to Kyle with a slow grin. "Looks like that undercover work will start a bit sooner than you'd expected.''

Chapter Four

In the foyer of the main house of the Lonesome Pony Ranch, Laura watched as the housekeeper left in search of Kyle Foster. Settling on a rustic bench, she renewed the debate she'd been having with herself all morning. She shouldn't have come. There was no real point in seeing the man again. She could have easily had C.J. deliver her packages, she reminded herself. She didn't need to get involved.

But she wanted to thank her rescuer again in person. And, just as important, she was curious to see if Kyle was as handsome as she remembered, or if the danger and emotion of that awful day had created his Greek-god effect in her mind, a figment that now haunted her imagination.

Once her curiosity was satisfied, she could return home and wipe him from her thoughts forever. She didn't have time for a handsome man. As she'd learned with Curt, they were nothing but trouble. Besides, keeping her father's lab running was a twenty-four-hour job.

C.J. had told her the Lonesome Pony had previously been a resort ranch. While Laura waited, she glanced around the cavernous, two-story room that must have served as a lobby and lounge for guests. The room's decorations were authentically Western, but in better taste than she'd expected of a former dude ranch. Lights from an elkhorn chandelier, suspended from the cathedral ceiling, banished the morning gloom. A fire crackling cheerfully in the massive fireplace constructed of local river rock provided a welcome buffer against the chill of the October day. High above the mantel, a moose head stared at her with woeful glass eyes, making her shiver and glance away. Scattered groupings of club chairs and deep, welcoming sofas, upholstered in either leather or a Navajo pattern, were arranged throughout the room in conversational clusters.

A grouping of framed pictures on the opposite wall caught her attention, and she crossed the room to examine them more closely. The sepia tones of the early twentieth-century photographs chronicled the area's history of railroads, cattle drives, rodeos and roundups.

"The days of the Wild, Wild West," a rich baritone voice spoke behind her.

Startled, she turned.

"It's still wild enough, from what I've seen the short year I've been here," Laura said.

Hands tucked in the back pockets of his jeans, Kyle Foster stood in the door to the hall, looking more appealing than she'd remembered. His tight, faded jeans accentuated slender hips, a plaid shirt deepened the forest green in his incredible eyes and a suede vest hung open over his powerful chest.

Thick hair, a sandy brown, fell across his high forehead, and her fingers itched with the urge to push it off his face.

His sudden and attractive appearance blew everything else from her thoughts.

Her mind went blank, and she couldn't think of anything else to say.

The killer grin she had recalled, vividly and accurately, after all, spread across his handsome face. "You wanted to see me?"

She nodded, returned to the bench where she'd left her packages and gathered them up. Overwhelming gratitude, she assured herself, was the reason for her kick-in-the-gut reaction to him.

Kyle stepped into the lounge and waved her toward the nearest group of club chairs. "Want some coffee? Dale always keeps a pot ready."

His welcome seemed genuinely friendly, but she found herself wanting to squirm under the intense scrutiny of those green eyes. She was certain he missed nothing about her, from the expensive cut of her gray wool slacks and the fine Irish stitches of her burgundy fisherman's sweater, to the flush of involuntary color that burned her cheeks.

She should have let C.J. run her errands. She was on the verge of making a fool of herself.

"No, thank you. I can't stay." She perched on the edge of a deep leather chair, ready for a quick getaway after she'd given him what she came for.

With a gracefulness unusual for a large man, Kyle dropped his tall frame easily into a chair angled beside hers.

"I'm glad you came." He leaned toward her, clasping his large, strong hands in front of him. Their cuts and scratches from the capitol wreckage had healed. "I've been wondering how you are."

She raised her head, looked into his sympathetic eyes, and saw more than courteous interest. His obvious concern flustered her more than his laser gaze. Mentally kicking herself, she wondered anew why she hadn't saved herself this emotional turmoil by letting C.J. run her errand.

"I'm doing…better." She sucked in a calming breath. "I miss Daddy terribly, but I have my memories and his work. They help."

Kyle nodded, the clean-shaven, square lines of his jaw set in a compassionate expression, a look that mirrored her own suffering, and she sensed that he understood the pain she'd endured since her father's murder. Judging from the anguish evident in his eyes, sometime in his past, Kyle Foster had apparently suffered, too.

His green gaze held hers for a long instant, until she realized she'd been staring. Lowering her glance to her lap, she remembered her packages. She picked up the one wrapped in brown paper and handed it to him.

"For me?" He raised his eyebrows in question. A crescent-shaped scar intersected his left eyebrow, and she wondered what had caused it. Not the capitol bombing. The crescent was an old wound, long healed.

At her nod, he ripped open the paper.

"It's your jacket. The denim one you gave me in the capitol."

She could still recall the warmth of the fabric as she'd slipped on the jacket that day, the inundation of pleasing fragrances of meadow grasses, leather and saddle soap that had engulfed her as if he'd wrapped his arms around her. With regret, she had laundered away the scent, because every time she had lifted the garment to her nose, it had brought back vivid images of the man who had risked his life to save hers.

Those vivid images had frequented her dreams, a bright oasis in the nightmare of her life the past few weeks.

She raised her eyes and found him looking at her so intently, she was certain he could read her thoughts. The heat increased in her cheeks.

"I should have returned it sooner," she said.

He shook his head. "You've had plenty to deal with."

She fought to keep alarm from showing on her face. Did he know about the break-in? The sheriff's department had insisted she tell no one about the theft of D-5 from the lab. They feared a statewide panic if the public got wind of the fact that a lethal biological weapon was in unknown hands.

"Settling an estate," he explained, almost is if he'd read her mind and was trying to ease her panic, "is never easy. Not only hard on the emotions, but it takes a devil of a lot of time."

She breathed a sigh of relief. The secret of the

D-5 theft was safe. Then she remembered her other package. "I wanted to thank you for saving my life."

"You already did. That night in the hospital."

She'd been so full of tranquilizers, she could barely remember his visit. She also had no idea what she'd said to him that night. "I don't remember."

"I remember." His voice was strong, rock steady.

"I wanted to show my gratitude for all you did." She thrust the wicker basket covered with a red-checkered napkin toward him. "But this is only a token. I couldn't think of anything to repay you adequately for risking your life for mine."

He lifted the napkin and peered beneath it. His face lit up with a warm smile so stunning it almost took her breath away. "Homemade cookies?"

"Chocolate-macadamia nut. They were Daddy's favorite."

He picked up a cookie and took a generous bite. A smile of pure pleasure wreathed his face. "Mmm. My mama would call these sin on a plate. Thank you."

"You're welcome." His delight in her gift generated a warm spot beneath her breastbone, dispelling some of the ice that had encased her heart since her father died. "I made extra, for Molly."

He had finished the cookie and was brushing crumbs from his hands. "You know about Molly?"

When he spoke his daughter's name, the tenderness in his expression and the affection in his voice left no doubt how smitten the man was with his daughter. He loved her and wasn't ashamed to show it.

"C.J. told me about Molly. She's crazy about her. Seems your little girl has quite an admiration society here at the ranch." And if the child was as charming as her father, Laura could well understand why.

"Would you like to meet her?"

Now was the time to make her getaway. She stood, opened her mouth to say she had to leave.

"I'd like that very much," came out instead.

WEARING THE FRESHLY laundered jacket Laura had just returned to him, Kyle stepped onto the broad front porch of the ranch with Laura beside him. It was one of those perfect autumn days with the sky an endless bowl of deep blue, broken only by the occasional chevron of geese, heading south for the winter. The cool air, mercifully unlike the L.A. smog, had the refreshing tang of a clear, crisp vintage Chardonnay. Along Crooked Creek, the leaves of aspen and cottonwood quivered golden in the light breeze, and the pasture that stretched before them was a crazy quilt of grasses, painted varying shades of brown and gold by a killing frost.

A perfect day.

Except for the fact that Laura's father was dead and the Black Order, armed with biological weapons, was still on the loose.

"Molly's around back, riding her pony." He gestured toward the porch steps, and Laura descended beside him. "You like horses?"

Laura nodded. "When I was a little girl, Daddy sent me to a boarding school back East. Horseback riding was part of the curriculum. But I haven't ridden since.''

They followed the gravel driveway around the main house to the corral beside the barn. Inside the fenced circle, Molly sat astride Ribbons, clutching the reins tightly in her petite hands, her tiny mouth set in concentration. Jewel rode beside her, ready to spring to the rescue if needed. Blond curls peeked from the bottom of the safety helmet he'd insisted Molly wear, despite the derision of Jewel, who thought helmets were for sissies, greenhorns and old ladies. Kyle didn't care if every hand on the ranch made fun of the helmet. Keeping Molly safe was his main concern.

Laura climbed the bottom railing of the corral and hooked her elbows over the top one. The breeze lifted her thick black hair away from the slender column of her throat, and the sunlight sparkled in the periwinkle blue of her eyes. At the sight of her, Kyle felt the stirrings of desire.

''She's adorable.'' Laura's face broke into a delighted smile as Molly walked her pony by.

''You won't get any argument from me,'' Kyle said. ''She has me wrapped around her little finger.''

As he watched the enjoyment spread across Laura's lovely features and the cold air deepen the color in her cheeks, he was glad he'd brought her to meet his daughter. He doubted she had smiled much in the past few weeks.

Molly completed the circuit and tugged on the reins, halting her pony in front of them. Jewel reined in her horse a distance away, ready to respond if Ribbons bolted.

"That's some fancy riding, doodlebug," Kyle said. "You're almost qualified for the rodeo."

Molly smiled with pride, forming deep dimples in her plump cheeks. "Jewel says I'm ready to trot."

Kyle motioned to Laura. "This is Miss Quinlan."

"Hi," Molly said. "Did you come to ride?"

Laura shook her head. "I came to meet you. What's your pony's name?"

Molly's Kewpie-doll mouth lifted in a mischievous grin. "Guess."

"Molly loves guessing games," Kyle explained.

"How many guesses do I get?" Laura asked.

Molly scrunched up her face, considering, then held up three pudgy fingers. "Free. And no fair helping, Daddy."

"I wouldn't dare," he said with a straight face. "But what's Miss Quinlan's prize if she guesses right?"

"A kiss," Molly said.

"You'll kiss me if I guess your pony's name?" Laura asked.

Molly shook her head. "No, *Daddy* will. He's the best kisser."

Kyle stifled a grin at the startled expression and subsequent flush on Laura's face. "Okay, Laura. Give it your best shot."

Laura thought for a moment. "Is it Dudley?"

Molly laughed. "No, Dudley's a silly name for a pony."

"Of course. I'll have to do better." Laura closed her eyes to concentrate.

Kyle noted the thick, black lashes lying long against her cheeks and hoped she managed to come up with the right answer. He wouldn't mind kissing Laura Quinlan. All in the spirit of Molly's game, of course.

Laura tried again. "Bigfoot?"

Molly shrieked with delighted laughter and shook her head.

Kyle cast Laura a teasing look. "I don't think you're really trying. Afraid you'll win?"

Her blue eyes flashed. "I *want* to win!"

He raised his eyebrows. "Hungry for one of my kisses?"

She flushed again, shook her head and stated primly, "I have an innate competitive streak."

"One more guess," Molly prompted her.

"Hmm." Laura wrinkled her forehead in thought. "This one will have to be good."

Kyle smiled at Molly. "Give her a hint, doodle-bug."

Molly turned to Laura. "You wear 'em in your hair."

Kyle looked at Laura. "You can't miss with a clue like that."

"Something you wear in your hair," Laura repeated. She threw Kyle a teasing glance. "That's easy. Your pony's name is Barrette."

"No," Molly squealed. "It's Ribbons."

"Darn." Laura snapped her fingers. "Why didn't I think of that?"

"Yeah, why didn't you?" A surprising wave of disappointment washed over him. He'd been looking forward to awarding Laura's prize.

Molly's smile crumpled. "I'm sorry you didn't win."

Laura reached across the rail and patted Molly's hand. "It's all right. I tried my best. That's what matters."

"I know." Molly's face brightened. "*I'll* give you a kiss."

Kyle's stomach flip-flopped at the yearning he saw on Laura's face. He'd known she liked kids. She'd been terrific with the schoolchildren trapped in the capitol. But now he could see the raw longing in her eyes. Here was a woman who should have children of her own. He wondered why she didn't.

"Lean over," Molly ordered.

Laura stood on tiptoe and stretched across the railing. Molly puckered her lips and planted a loud kiss on Laura's rosy cheek.

"Now," Molly said in what Kyle realized was an imitation of his own condolences to his daughter. "All better?"

"Much." Laura's eyes sparkled, but Kyle couldn't tell if tears or sunshine caused the shimmer.

"Molly," Jewel shouted from across the corral. "You gonna ride or sit there jawing all morning?"

Molly looked to Kyle. "Have to go, Daddy. Bye, Miss Kwin—" She scrunched her face as she struggled over Laura's last name.

"Call me Laura."

"Bye, Laura. If you come back, we can play another game."

"I'd like that." Laura watched Molly ride away, the stark hunger still on her face.

"You like kids," Kyle said.

As if embarrassed by how much her expression had given away, Laura composed her features. "I do, and I especially like Molly. She's delightful."

He waved to Molly again and turned away from the corral. "I always thought so, but then I'm biased."

Laura glanced at her watch. "It's late. I should get back to the lab."

"Miss Quinlan—"

"Laura."

"Okay, Laura. If you can spare me a few more minutes, I have something important to discuss with you."

"Sounds serious."

"It is."

"But I really have work—"

"It concerns your father's killers."

Her lovely features paled, and her delicate jaw set in determination. "You know who they are?"

"We can talk in my cabin."

She raised a dark, feathered eyebrow. "Why can't we talk here?"

He nodded toward the ranch hands coming and going as they exercised horses, mucked out the stables and herded their charges toward the pastures. "Too many ears."

"Well..."

"If you're worried about your honor, I'll leave the door open," he said with a wicked grin.

She smiled and shook her head. "That won't be necessary. C.J. says you're a man to be trusted."

"I appreciate the endorsement." He took her elbow and steered her gently toward one of the large cabins that ringed the swimming pool. "Molly and I take most of our meals at the main house, but we call this cabin home."

He led her up the steps to the wide front porch of the log cabin, opened the door and stepped aside for her to enter. Following her inside, he saw his living quarters as if through her eyes. The large, open room served as living room, dining room and kitchenette. Two bedrooms, divided by a bathroom, opened off the rear.

Molly's toys were scattered on the floor, newspapers littered the coffee table, and one of his shirts hung on the back of a chair. Moving with lightning speed, he kicked a path clear through the toys, scooped up the papers and shirt. After depositing his armload in his bedroom and closing the door, he turned back to Laura.

"Sorry for the mess. We weren't expecting company."

"No need to apologize. I won't faint over a little clutter. Daddy always—" She bit her bottom lip as if holding back her words, and the pained look returned to her eyes.

She'd been brave in the bombed-out building, and Kyle could see that she was being brave now, accepting the terrible burden of loss, keeping her magnificent head high, in spite of the bruised look around her eyes and the delicate slope of her shoulders.

He waved her to a seat on the sofa that matched the ones in the main house and slid into a chair across from her.

She lifted her head and summery blue eyes focused on him like magnets. "What about Daddy's killers?"

He leaned toward her, aching to take her hands in his, wanting to ease her pain. "It's a long story."

"Then you'd better start at the beginning."

"I'm not a cowboy."

"What?"

If the situation had been less grim, he might have laughed at her confusion, but the situation was critical. Josiah Quinlan had been murdered, terrorists had their hands on one of the most lethal biological weapons ever invented and Laura had a traitor working in her lab. Kyle needed her help to smoke him out and bring the Black Order to justice.

"None of us here are really cowboys. Frank's ex-military, Court's ex-FBI and I'm a former cop from Los Angeles."

Her eyes clouded with confusion. "But this ranch, the horses—"

"Daniel Austin bought this ranch as a base of operations for our group of undercover agents for the Department of Public Safety."

She shook her head, dazed by the news. "And no one else knows?"

"Not even the hands who work here. Only the

foreman, Patrick McMurty, and his wife and grand-daughter are aware of our real purpose.''

''And C.J.?''

Kyle nodded. ''Frank didn't just happen to be on that plane with C.J. He'd been sent to protect her.''

''Protect her from whom?''

''Everything I'm telling you is confidential. If not, more people could die.''

She nodded solemnly.

''There's a terrorist organization called the Black Order operating in the United States.''

''I've never heard of them.''

''Not many have—yet. The group's home base is the Middle Eastern Emirate of Agar. Their head-quarters are hidden in the mountain caves of that country. Although the emir professes not to endorse their actions, he also does nothing to catch them, either.''

''And their purpose?''

He admired her coolheadedness, her grasp of what was important. ''They're religious and political zeal-ots who despise Western ideology. Their primary purpose is to wreak havoc and destruction among their enemies.''

''Like the capitol bombing.'' Her voice sounded raw with pain.

''That was only a diversion. Their major purpose is to obtain biological weapons of mass destruction.''

Her eyes widened, and she started to speak but didn't.

''It's okay,'' he said. ''We know about the theft of the D-5.''

"And you think the Black Order took it?" Horror etched her face. She knew what D-5 could do, and now she knew the ruthlessness of the terrorists who'd stolen it.

"We're almost positive. Remember when C.J.'s plane went down, the one bringing her to work at the Quinlan Institute?"

Laura nodded. "A terrible—" She paused, awareness lighting her face. "It wasn't an accident, was it?"

"Gilad, a member of the Black Order, wanted to kidnap C.J., to force her to share her knowledge of biological weapons with their group, to prevent her from helping the Institute to develop antidotes and vaccines."

Laura seemed in shock. She'd already suffered so much, he wished for a merciful way to tell her, but the truth was too ugly to go down easy.

"You knew the plane accident was going to happen?" she asked.

"Not for sure. We sent Frank to take care of her, just in case."

Laura smiled. "He more than took care of her. He fell in love with her."

Kyle was happy to see her smile return, like the sun coming out after a rainy day. "Frank's a lucky guy."

Laura's happy expression faded fast. "Daddy received warnings weeks ago to tighten security. He did all he could, but he didn't have the funds to provide all the safeguards he wanted."

Kyle reached across and grasped her hands. Her

icy fingers didn't resist. "We need your help, Laura."

She lifted her chin, her mouth open with surprise. "*My* help? I know nothing about tracking terrorists."

Kyle gripped her cold hands tighter. "We think the Black Order has an accomplice, someone working inside the Institute."

She yanked her hands from his and turned away, denial evident in her posture. "That can't be. Daddy thoroughly checked the background of everyone on the staff."

"I'm sure he did," Kyle said placatingly. "But people can change."

"Change? What are you saying?"

"Bribery or blackmail has led many good people astray."

She shook her head. "I can't believe it. I *won't* believe it. It's too horrible."

Kyle stood, grasped her slender shoulders and lifted her to her feet. She was only a few inches shorter than his five foot eleven, so he had to dip his head only slightly to stare straight into her breathtaking blue eyes. "The theft had to be an inside job."

She turned her head to avoid his piercing gaze. "But they came in from the outside, cut the fence, forced the lock—"

Catching hold of her chin, he turned her face toward his. "But once inside, they knew exactly where to go to find what they needed. *Someone* gave them directions."

She sank back into her chair. "If that's true—"

"Believe it, Laura. There's no other explanation."

"Then the traitor's still there."

He nodded. "That's where you come in."

"You want *me* to catch him?"

Kyle knelt beside her. "Catching him is our job. But we can't do it from the outside. I'm asking your permission to work at the lab undercover."

She looked at him as if he'd lost his mind.

Chapter Five

Kyle knocked on the door of Daniel's study and stuck his head inside.

Daniel, flipping through a file at his desk, waved the younger man in. "Miss Quinlan gone?"

Kyle nodded. "Just left."

"Did she agree?"

"Not yet."

"Will she?"

Kyle slumped into a deep chair in front of the desk and pushed his fingers through his hair. "I think she's in shock. The idea of a traitor in the lab coming hard on the heels of her father's death really shook her up. She said she'd think about the undercover bit and let me know."

"Did you stress that time is crucial?"

"I tried."

Daniel leaned back in his chair and laced his fingers across his powerful chest. "Laura Quinlan's a good woman. I'll have C.J. talk to her, see if she can bring her around. We need you inside that lab, Kyle. The sooner, the better."

"I agree. I'll plan accordingly, so I can move fast once we get her approval."

Daniel nodded. "I've been looking over your file. You attended UCLA?"

"It seems a long time ago now. Double-majored in chemistry and biology."

"And earned a doctorate in chemistry. How'd you end up in police work?"

Daniel's question brought back memories of agonizing over his decision. "Science fascinated me, but I wanted to work with people. Guess you could say I got lonesome working mainly with rats."

His reasons went much deeper, but he didn't want to go into them now.

Daniel grinned. "Think of the Black Order as bigger, deadlier rats. Let's hope we nail those bastards."

Kyle remembered Laura and Jeremy and the little girls trapped by their bomb. "Nothing would make me happier."

Daniel leaned forward, his smile gone. "I don't want any more deaths."

Kyle nodded. Daniel knew what he was talking about. The boss himself had worked undercover with Texas Confidential for fifteen years. Last year he'd come close to infiltrating the Calderone/Rialto drug cartel when he'd been ambushed and disappeared. Everyone, including his ex-wife, Sherry, and their twelve-year-old son, Jessie, had thought him dead. Long before that case, the trauma of undercover work had already placed too high an emotional burden on their family, and Daniel and Sherry had divorced.

Kyle glanced at the framed picture on the credenza behind Daniel's desk. Sherry, an attractive woman with thick chestnut hair and laughing brown eyes sat with her arms around Jessie, who looked like a boy-ish version of his father. Daniel rarely spoke of his family, but Kyle had often seen the loneliness and longing in his boss's eyes when he gazed at that pic-ture.

"I've asked Court to check with the Bureau," Daniel said. "You'll need unshakable credentials. Once you show up at the Institute, I'm sure the traitor in their midst will check you out."

"What's my cover story?"

Daniel tapped the file folder on his desk with a slender finger. "The FBI will plant records at UCLA, in case anyone inquires, that show you working as a researcher there from your undergraduate days to the present. That background should keep you safe enough."

Safe enough for himself, Kyle thought, but not for Molly. "Laura says security isn't as tight as her fa-ther wanted, due to monetary restraints. I can't take Molly into a dangerous situation." His gut clenched, torn between wanting his daughter with him and keeping her safe.

"I understand," Daniel said. "Dale and Jewel can take care of her here, and you can visit when you can. Having C.J. as a colleague gives you an excuse to drop in at the ranch."

Kyle nodded in agreement, but his heart wasn't in it. Molly had been through so much. First her mother's desertion, then the move to Montana. He hated leaving her, even for a few days at a time, but he knew how important this undercover assignment was. Finding the traitor in the lab was the agents' best chance at tracking down the Black Order. If they didn't, thousands of little girls like Molly could die horrible deaths. He had no choice but to leave her, as much as it galled him.

"I'll need to bone up on the current research at the Institute," he said.

Daniel nodded. "I'll ask C.J. to bring you as much information as she can without casting suspicion on herself. And I'll have one of the hands cover your ranch duties to give you time to study and prepare."

Kyle pushed to his feet. "All we need now is the green light from Laura Quinlan."

Daniel nodded, his expression grim. "And a hell of a lot of luck."

LAURA DROPPED the letter from the insurance company onto her father's desk, not knowing whether to laugh or cry at the irony. The enclosed check for two million dollars, the death benefit, fluttered to the floor. Her father's life insurance policy now provided the funds to keep the Institute in full operation.

Fighting back tears, she retrieved the check, locked it in the office safe and silently renewed her vow to continue his work. That and bringing his killers to justice would keep her going, in spite of her pain.

At loose ends, she wandered aimlessly through the empty rooms of the director's house at the Quinlan Institute, the home she had shared with her father.

After returning from the Lonesome Pony this morning, she'd spent the last few hours on correspondence, writing dozens of thank-you notes for flowers and messages of condolence. Then she'd prepared a mass mailing to all her father's professional associates, assuring them that the work of the Institute would continue, even without Josiah Quinlan at the helm.

A gurgling in her stomach reminded her she hadn't eaten all day. Grief had stolen her appetite, but she forced herself to head for the kitchen. Even if she wasn't hungry, she'd need her strength to maintain her father's work.

Golden beams of October sunlight poured through the tall windows of the big kitchen and reflected off the sand-colored granite of the countertops and the bright lemon yellow of the walls. She'd loved this room with its pale maple cabinets and terra-cotta tiled floor the minute she first saw it. Her father had suggested they hire a cook and a housekeeper, but Laura had refused. As much as she enjoyed her public relations work for the Institute, she loved homemaking more.

She supposed some women would call her crazy, but she was happiest either in the kitchen preparing a special meal or performing the myriad chores that kept the elegant Western-style chalet sparkling.

But that had been before her father died. With no one for her to take care of, the house, and especially the sunny kitchen, mocked her now with its emptiness.

A house needed family, she thought, and remembered Molly Foster's charming giggles. Her heart ached for a child of her own, a shield against the loneliness, but her head reminded her of her responsibilities. She had to pick up where her father had left off, assuming many of the administrative tasks he'd tackled in addition to his research. She had no time for a family of her own.

And no time for contemplating a handsome not-cowboy named Kyle Foster, who'd set her pulse racing with his killer smile and dancing eyes that mirrored a sharp intellect and hints of a sense of humor.

If she agreed to his undercover assignment, she'd have to avoid him if she intended to get any work done. The emotion she'd tagged as simple gratitude was beginning to feel too much like attraction. She should squelch that feeling fast. She didn't have time for the distraction.

And even if she had time, she didn't have the courage to risk her heart again. Not after what Curt had done to her.

She found herself standing in front of the stainless-steel refrigerator door, hand on the handle, staring blankly into space. She'd forgotten that she'd come to the kitchen to eat. While removing lettuce, tomato and cold cuts from the refrigerator, she replayed in her thoughts her earlier conversation with Kyle. She'd been stunned to discover he wasn't a cowboy, but an undercover government agent.

Looking back, she should have guessed something was strange when none of the media coverage of the capitol bombing had carried pictures or even mentioned the name of her rescuer. Heroes like Kyle were usually snapped up and interviewed on the *Today* show. She'd been too devastated by her father's death to notice Kyle's lack of notoriety until now. It made sense. A man working undercover couldn't have his face splashed across the front of every newspaper and television screen in the country.

Even more shocking than his cowboy masquerade had been his allegation that someone at the Institute was in league with foreign terrorists, had helped them steal the D-5. As she assembled a sandwich on whole-grain bread, she struggled over whether to accept Kyle's request and wished her father was there to give advice.

"Science can be a savior or a monster," she recalled Josiah saying in his moving speech to the employees the day the Institute opened. "It can be used for unlimited good or unspeakable horror. The purpose of our Institute is to block the efforts of those who would bend science to their own evil purpose."

Remembering his words, she had no doubt what her father's answer to Kyle Foster's request would be.

Leaving her sandwich untouched on the kitchen island, she returned to her father's office. In his address book, she found the telephone number of the Lonesome Pony and placed her call.

"Ms. McMurty," she said when Dale answered. "Tell Kyle Foster I want to see him. I'll be there within the hour."

KYLE PERCHED on the porch railing of the main house and watched the black sport-utility vehicle leave a trail of dust on the road from the highway as it approached the ranch. Even at a distance, the silver lettering of the Quinlan Research Institute was visible on the doors. Laura Quinlan had apparently reached a decision about his undercover job in her lab, but the fact that she'd decided so damn fast made him nervous.

A quick no was always easiest.

If she turned down the request, he didn't know what would disappoint him more, the roadblock in their search for the Black Order or the fact that he'd no longer have an excuse to spend time with a woman he couldn't seem to banish from his thoughts.

He recognized the thrumming of his nerves, the adrenaline rush coursing through his veins at her approach. That hyped-up, ready-to-fight feeling always took over when a dangerous task loomed ahead of him. But the other sensation, the heady anticipation of spending time with her again, was a feeling he hadn't experienced in a long time.

Too long.

Damn. He had to get his emotions under control.

His preoccupation with Josiah Quinlan's pretty daughter was not only *not* smart, it could be fatal. Undercover assignments were always hazardous, and an intriguing distraction like Laura could get him—and others—killed.

Her car pulled to a stop in the parking area. Laura hopped out, dressed as she'd been that morning, with the addition of a gray suede jacket against the growing chill. He couldn't tell whether the increasing cold or emotion had heightened the color in her cheeks, but her blue eyes flashed with determination, and her delicate mouth was set in a firm line.

She wasn't smiling.

Not a good sign.

Kyle climbed down from his perch on the railing and walked to meet her.

"Didn't think I'd see you again so soon," he said.

With hands jammed in the pockets of her jacket, she met his gaze without flinching. "I've made up my mind."

He gave a cautious shake of his head and lowered his voice. "Let's not talk here. Voices carry."

"Sorry." She blushed in embarrassment. "I'm not used to this."

He took her elbow and steered her toward the hitching rail in front of the main house. When the housekeeper had called to announce Laura's coming, he'd gone to the barn and saddled horses. His own Appaloosa and a gentle bay mare stood waiting, their warm breath misting in the cold air.

"You're here for a horseback ride, aren't you?" he suggested with a lifted eyebrow.

Laura caught on to the charade immediately, reminding him that she was not only beautiful, but intelligent as well. "I've been looking forward to riding again ever since we moved to Montana. I just haven't taken the time until now."

"I think you'll like the bay. Her name's Sugar. She's easy to handle with a good disposition."

Kyle untied Sugar's reins and held her head while Laura mounted with a graceful swing. He untied Flash and climbed into his own saddle.

"Which way?" Laura asked.

He glanced to the sky where low, leaden clouds portending snow scudded in quickly from the west. "We'll head for the creek. It's not too far from shelter, in case the weather worsens."

With an expertness he couldn't help admiring after his own trials and torments in learning to ride, Laura turned Sugar toward the creek. Kyle did the same with Flash and settled in at a trot alongside her.

Once they were a good distance from the main house, she glanced across at him. "You handle a horse like a pro. Thought you said you weren't a cowboy."

He flicked her a grin. "I had to learn. Spent a lot of time on heating pads and coated with Ben-Gay when I first arrived. Before then, my closest encounters with horses were reruns of *Mr. Ed.*"

She smiled then, not a full smile, but a ghost of one that lifted the corners of her full mouth slightly. She'd been through so much pain recently, he'd give anything to make her laugh.

For the next ten minutes, they worked their way across the broad pasture between the ranch house and the creek. Dead grass crunched beneath the horses' hooves. At one point, a ruffled grouse, startled by their approach, flew up almost beneath Sugar's nose with a frightened cry. The bay shied, but Laura maintained her seat and control of the mare.

"You're much better at riding than I am," he said with admiration in his voice.

She shrugged. "Like I said, I rode often at boarding school. I guess it's like riding a bicycle. Once you learn, you never forget."

"I hope so," he said with a rueful smile. "I don't think my backside could handle having to learn again."

This time her smile broadened and lit her face for an instant before her expression sobered again. With a skillful nudge of her knees, she coaxed the mare into a run and galloped ahead of him toward the trees that lined the creek.

For a moment, Kyle watched her go, admiring the way her slender behind held the saddle, the graceful posture of her back, the way the wind tossed her thick black hair behind her.

Pure, unadulterated lust poured through him, and he silently chastised himself for it. Laura Quinlan was a sweet, gentle woman who had recently suffered the loss of her only living relative. She didn't need the irritation of some horny male trying to put the make on her. She needed courtesy, respect and kindness.

He groaned inwardly.

All he wanted was to kiss her, but that wouldn't be wise. Not for her, and damn well not for his undercover investigation.

Reining in his desire, he kicked Flash into a gallop and followed.

Laura pulled up at the tree line and waited for him. With her hair tousled from the wind, her lips and cheeks rosy from exertion and the cold, she looked even more alluring than she had when she arrived. He maneuvered Flash alongside her and folded his hands, hands that itched to touch her, on the pommel of his saddle.

"It's beautiful here." She gazed at the creek, rushing over its rocky bed at their feet, widening to calm pools just past them, where aspen leaves floated, flecks of gold in the clear water.

With a worried glance at the approaching cold front, Kyle cut straight to the matter at hand. "You said you'd made up your mind. Can I work undercover at the lab or not?"

"Yes." She turned slightly in the saddle to face him. "But only on my terms."

The thrumming of his nerves increased, and he wanted to shake her. Didn't she know how much was at stake? Why was she throwing roadblocks in his path? "Guess I'd better hear those terms before we clinch this deal."

She turned up the collar of her jacket against the growing wind, calling attention to the slender column of her neck. "My father's life insurance benefits arrived today. There's enough money now to increase security and keep the Institute's programs running."

"That's good, isn't it?"

She nodded. "But I know nothing about security."

"Daniel can put you in touch with a good firm—"

"No."

"No?"

"I want *you* to oversee protection of the Institute."

"My cover is as a research scientist. Taking over security would call too much attention to me."

She thrust her chin forward at a determined angle,

but her full lips quivered slightly, and tears darkened the blue of her eyes. "You're the only one I trust."

"Let's be reasonable about this." He forced a gentle tone to hide his exasperation. "If I agreed to oversee security, I'd simply call Daniel for his help. You'd have the same results in the long run."

"I'll feel safer with you in charge."

He leaned across the space between them and laid his hand on her gloved ones, crossed on the saddle horn. "We can't always have what we want. I want to keep Molly with me at the Institute, but I can't."

She made no effort to hide her disappointment. "Why not? We have an excellent day-care center—"

"I won't place my daughter in jeopardy."

"But if you hired the right security, she'd be safe."

Kyle swung out of the saddle, tied Flash's reins to a nearby tree and held out his arms to Laura. "Let's walk."

She slid from her horse into his arms with ease, and he restrained himself from pulling her close. Her scent, a floral mixture much like the orange blossoms of his youth, tantalized his senses, and he forced himself to take a step back instead of gathering her against him.

After securing her horse, he led her to a path that edged the creek, broad enough for the two to walk side by side. A sharp wind from the northwest blew at their backs and scattered a carpet of falling leaves ahead of them.

"You mentioned terms," Kyle said. "What other conditions did you have in mind?"

"You wanted to come undercover as a researcher. What I really need right now is an administrator."

"Whoa!" Kyle came to a quick stop. "Haven't you been listening? Undercover means inconspicuous, unobtrusive, not calling any attention to oneself. If I come in as the head honcho, every person at the Institute will scrutinize the daylights out of me."

She lifted her chin and gave him a shy smile. "I admit I don't know much about undercover work, but isn't there a saying that often you can hide something best in plain sight?"

"Like me, taking charge? That's crazy."

She placed her hand on his sleeve, frankness lighting her face. "Daddy's authority was unquestioned when he was alive. Since his death, several of the scientists have been openly vying for control. With all the infighting going on, it's hurting progress in our research. If you come in as our administrator, that's one conflict solved."

Kyle shook his head. "And I'll have made several enemies right off the bat. They'll wonder what right I, a newcomer and outsider, have to take over when they've worked with your father for years. Not only the terrorist collaborator but every other would-be administrator will be researching my background with a fine-tooth comb."

They had reached a large outcropping of granite. Laura sank onto the rock, shoulders slumped, eyes downcast. "I thought I'd figured it all out. It seemed like a perfect solution to both our problems."

Kyle settled beside her, longing to pull her into his arms and comfort her, but he kept his distance. Too much desire fought against his better nature for him to take a chance on touching her. His reassuring hug might turn into something deeper, wilder.

The last thing he wanted was to frighten her.

"Just hire me on as a simple researcher and let me start right away. The insider in your lab is our best hope of finding the Black Order before they decide to use that D-5 on innocent people."

She stooped, picked up a pebble from the path and pitched it into a calm section of the creek. It landed with a plop, sending concentric ripples across the water's surface, tossing the floating leaves like tiny boats in a squall. When she turned to face him again, her expression was calm, but just as somber and resolute as earlier.

"There's only one way to do this and both get what we want," she said.

He smiled at her earnestness. "If you've thought of a solution that solves both our problems, you're a miracle worker."

"It will work, all right." Her solemn eyes sought his and held his gaze. "But there's just one catch."

"Which is?"

"You'll have to marry me."

Chapter Six

At the word *marry,* his gut tightened as if caught in a vise.

"Been there, done that." The protest was out of his mouth before Kyle could think. "Didn't work the first time. I don't want to hit that slippery slope again."

Laura cocked her head and looked at him, the corner of her mouth quirked in an ironic smile. Noting the shrewdness in her eyes, Kyle shook his head in embarrassment.

"You're not talking about a *real* marriage, are you?" he said.

Her expression sobered. "It would have to be legal, to safeguard your cover, but it would be in name only. Just for the sake of appearances."

In name only.

Memories of Alicia flooded him. Their last year of marriage, the year after Molly was born, might as well have been in name only. And it hadn't all been Alicia's fault. He should have been more understanding. When he'd joined the bomb squad and his job had become even more dangerous than that of a cop on street patrol, she'd pulled away. He'd seen the fear in her eyes every time he'd left the house, but he hadn't known what to do about it. Her fear of losing him, especially after he'd had too many close calls, had driven a wedge between them. Alicia had begun to distance herself, almost as if preparing for the worst.

He had responded in kind. Unable to alleviate her fears, he, too, had pulled away, until they were strangers living in the same house, with only Molly keeping them together. When Alicia finally stormed out, Kyle had been surprised but not devastated.

And he'd been angry for Molly's sake.

But the love he and Alicia had shared, the passion that had created his beautiful daughter, had died long before Alicia walked out the door.

Although he understood the reasons for the demise of his marriage, failure hurt, and he'd promised himself he'd never make that mistake again. As long as he was in law enforcement, he couldn't be involved with a woman. Couldn't spare the time to build and maintain a relationship. Couldn't risk the distraction loving a woman could cause in his work.

He shook himself from his memories to find Laura staring at him, a frown creasing the smooth perfection of her forehead.

"I'm not used to proposing." Her voice was light, her expression grim. "And you're not making it any easier for me."

Kyle buried his emotions deep inside and tried to look at Laura simply as a colleague, his partner in tracking down the Black Order. "I don't see how us

being married—in name only, of course—solves the
problems at the Institute.''

"It gives you the best reason in the world to be
there, as my husband. And who better to administer
my father's institute? Who better to oversee security
than the man I marry? Who could question that?''

He removed his Stetson and shoved his fingers
through his hair. "Lots of folks.''

She shook her head. "I don't think so.''

He knew what he was about to say would hurt her,
so he gentled his voice. "The first question they'll
ask is *why* you decided to marry so soon after your
father's death.''

She flinched at his words, and tears glistened in
her eyes, but she pulled herself up straight and lifted
her chin, as if in defiance. "I'll tell them I couldn't
stand the loneliness. Everyone at the Institute knows
how close Daddy and I were. They'll understand.''

Kyle could see all too clearly the truth in her statement. Once again, he fought the urge to draw her
into his arms and comfort her. She was obviously
struggling so hard to be brave that he doubted she'd
appreciate his concern.

"The next question they'll ask,'' he said in a sympathetic tone, "is who is Kyle Foster? No one will
have heard of or seen me before.''

Her smile banished the tears from her eyes. "I've
already thought of the answer to that one. I can say
I'd met you several times over the years at various
conventions and seminars. That we've exchanged let-
ters, talked on the phone, and were planning to marry
in the spring. Since Daddy's gone—'' her voice

broke slightly, and this time he couldn't resist reaching for her hands "—we moved up our wedding date so I wouldn't be alone and you could help me run the Institute."

"You think they'll believe you?" Even through her suede gloves, he could feel the heat from her hands, a warmth that only fueled his urge to hold her close.

"C.J. can help spread the news. Since she and I have been friends, everyone will assume I confided in her earlier and now she's free to share that information."

"That takes care of your problems," he said. "But what about mine?"

"Molly?"

He nodded. He had already figured out the answer, but her tactics had impressed him so far, and he wanted to hear the solution Laura would come up with.

"With you overseeing security, you can make special provisions for Molly's safety, both at the house and the day-care center."

"That makes sense."

"And—" Laura broke off with a blush.

"And what?"

"Since she'll be living with us, there'll be two of us to watch out for her."

The longing look in her periwinkle eyes Kyle had noted that morning when Laura met Molly had reappeared. "You like kids, don't you?"

"Guilty as charged." Laura lifted her lips in a

genuine smile that momentarily chased the grief from her eyes. "Molly's a sweetheart."

Paternal pride filled him. "She has that effect on everybody."

"With Molly living with us, your cover's even more secure. Who would expect a spy to bring his daughter on assignment with him?"

Kyle stood and slapped his thigh with his hat. "Exactly. Can't you see how crazy this whole scheme sounds?"

With a sigh of resignation, she rose to her feet and walked toward Sugar. Halfway there, she turned. "I confess I know nothing about the kind of work you do, and I'm possibly way off base with my suggestion. But I think it can work. Will you at *least* think about it?"

He jammed on his Stetson and strode toward his horse. "I don't have time for leisurely contemplation. Every minute advances the Black Order closer to using that D-5."

She didn't move. Snowflakes tumbled from the sky and caught like shimmering white jewels in the black tangle of her hair. "Is that a yes?"

"No."

Her face fell. "Then there's nothing more to discuss."

"Oh yes there is. We're going to talk your whole crazy scheme over with Daniel as soon as we get back to the main house."

She hurried to the bay, leaped into the saddle and urged the horse close to him. "Then it's a definite maybe?"

Indecision tore his insides six ways to Sunday. He wanted to catch the Black Order, he wanted Molly with him. And, God help him, the thought of being Laura's husband, even if only pretending, was more enticing than he dared admit. He needed Daniel's cool head and clear wisdom to keep him from making a terrible mistake. If Daniel thought the scheme would fly, then Kyle would accept the risks.

He turned his horse toward the main house. "Let's talk to Daniel first."

LAURA BENT HER HEAD BACK to look up at the sky-scraper that was the Orange County courthouse, its glass windows glistening in the afternoon light. Two days ago, riding Sugar back to the main house at the Lonesome Pony, she'd been blinded by snow. Today she squinted in the brightness of the hot California sun. Because Kyle's cover was that he worked as a scientist in L.A., they'd decided to be married there.

"Smile for the camera," Frank called from below them on the courthouse steps.

"Righto." With that cheery British encouragement, C.J. stood grinning at her husband's elbow as he adjusted the focus on his Nikon. "Happy the bride the sun shines on."

"If she doesn't melt," Laura muttered under her breath as perspiration slid between her shoulder blades.

Beside her, Kyle laughed, draped his arm over her shoulders and pulled her close. "Just a few quick shots for the folks back home. Then we'll get out of this heat."

With her bouquet of orange blossoms and steph-
anotis wilting in her hands, she flashed what she
hoped was an ecstatic matrimonial grin for the camera.

It hadn't been what she'd call a fairy-tale wedding.
Frank and C.J. had stood as their witnesses. The
judge's chambers were small and cluttered and
reeked of cigar smoke, in spite of L.A.'s anti-
smoking laws. The judge himself, a small, squat,
balding man with a physique like the proverbial fire
hydrant beneath his wrinkled robes, had mumbled the
minimum necessary to bind them legally. She
doubted the disheveled old magistrate had a senti-
mental or romantic bone in his body.

And when he'd pronounced them man and wife,
Kyle's kiss had been as reserved and impersonal as
a stranger's.

She suppressed a hysterical giggle. Kyle *was* a
stranger. She should have her head examined, marrying a man she barely knew.

But, God help her, in spite of that fact, when his
lips had brushed hers at the end of the ceremony,
she'd wanted more. She'd wanted his strong arms
around her, lifting her off her feet, driving away the
heartache and loneliness with the heat of his kisses.

Kyle squeezed her shoulder, and she turned to find
him staring at her, concern in his jade eyes. "You
okay?"

He'd caught her daydreaming, and her face, already red from the heat, flushed even more. "Just
too hot."

Recalling her lustful thoughts, the double meaning

of her comment hit her. She could only hope Kyle
wasn't a mind reader.

"Let's get out of this sun." Grasping her elbow,
and apparently unaware of his effect on her, he led
her down the stairs into the shade of a ligustrum tree
where Frank and C.J. waited.

"Ready to fly back?" Kyle asked.

Early that morning, the four had left Gallatin Field
near Bozeman in a small jet Frank had chartered
from Sunbird Aviation for the trip to L.A. With the
wedding over, they had time to fly back to Montana
before nightfall.

"Aren't you forgetting something?" Frank's
broad grin qualified as a leer.

"We have the marriage license—" Kyle patted
the breast pocket of his navy blue suit, then nodded
toward Frank's camera "—and the wedding photos,
so we're all set."

"Nope." Frank shook his head. "Not yet."

C.J.'s smile was as leering as her husband's.
"Whoever heard of a wedding without a honeymoon?"

Laura's knees threatened to give way, and she
sank onto a concrete bench. "A honeymoon wasn't
part of the deal. We only brought our luggage in case
there was a delay getting the license."

Kyle ran a finger beneath the stiff white collar of
his dress shirt. "Laura's right. We should head back
now. The sooner I'm in at the Institute, the sooner
we find our man."

"The heat's addling your brains, bud." Frank
grinned again, and Laura resisted the urge to swat

the smirk off his handsome face. "If anyone decides to check out the authenticity of this marriage, you want it to look real, don't you?"

Kyle grimaced. "Sure, but—"

"No buts," Frank said. "I've reserved a suite for you at the LAX Hilton. Had your luggage sent there from the plane. You and Laura should go there now. We'll fly out at eight tomorrow morning."

Laura was glad she was sitting down. The prospect of spending the night in a hotel room, in such proximity to the man who was now legally her husband, made her head spin.

"What about you two?" Kyle asked Frank.

Frank held up the camera. "We'll get this film developed. C.J. will do a little shopping. I have some errands to run for Daniel. Then we have a suite of our own reserved."

"Why don't you join us for dinner?" Laura asked, hoping to minimize her time alone with Kyle. She knew they'd be living together at the Institute, but the director's house was huge, with lots of bedrooms. Enough for her and Kyle to have plenty of personal space. Unlike the intimacy of a hotel suite.

C.J. shook her head. "You two should order something elegant and romantic from room service. If you were true newlyweds, you wouldn't poke your noses outside that suite from now until we leave tomorrow."

Frank handed Kyle a set of keys. "Take the rental car. We'll call a taxi."

Before Laura could think of a suitable protest, the couple turned and headed toward the street.

"Looks like we're stuck with each other." Kyle's expression was rueful.

"Now *that's* a promising premise on which to start a marriage," Laura joked, hoping humor would stop the butterflies from diving like kamikazes in her stomach.

His answering grin was warm and friendly. "Daniel said this marriage was a good idea. He didn't say it would be easy."

She relaxed. Kyle Foster was a good and decent man. He'd treat her like a lady, so what was she worried about?

That he'd treat her like a lady when she wanted to be treated like a lover.

That rebellious thought propelled her to her feet. Squelching the desire that gripped her as she gazed at her new husband, as deliciously attractive in a suit and tie as in jeans, she motioned toward the parking lot where they'd left the rental car. "Let's get this honeymoon on the road."

Lifting his left eyebrow, the one with the tiny crescent-shaped scar, he reached for her hand. They raced down the sidewalk and laughed together when Laura tossed her bouquet to a group of female office workers apparently returning to the courthouse from lunch. Like sharks in a feeding frenzy, the women scrambled for the prize, but Laura and Kyle didn't wait to see the victor.

Driving back to the airport, they both were silent. They listened to the radio while Kyle wove in and out of six-lane traffic with the experienced ease of an L.A. commuter. Watching the maniacal antics of

California drivers should have occupied Laura's thoughts, but visions of Kyle with her, alone in a honeymoon suite, drove everything else from her mind.

Kyle pulled up in front of the Hilton and handed the car keys to the valet. The attack of nerves that hit her when she stepped out of the car couldn't have been worse if she'd been a virgin bride.

Kyle took her hand, leaned forward as if to kiss her and whispered in her ear, "Smile. You're on your honeymoon, not death row."

Playing the part, she flung her arms around his neck and kissed him on the lips. The resulting heat that rocketed through her made the California sun feel like a cold snap. She pulled back, flustered.

Kyle's eyes glowed with approval, but whether of her impromptu performance or her kissing, she couldn't tell.

"That's more like it." Kyle tucked her arm through his and gave her hand an approving pat.

Together they crossed the lobby to the desk, claimed their key and entered the elevator. She was grateful for the crowd, even in the elevator, because she didn't know what to say. She'd have to get used to their charade, used to pretend kisses and fake terms of endearment if they were to convince the Institute staff they were truly married.

But she mustn't become so accustomed to being Kyle's wife that she'd be sorry when the masquerade ended. She'd been terribly hurt when her marriage with Curt had failed. She'd have to guard herself from Kyle's seductive charm so she could walk away with no regrets.

The doors of the elevator opened on their floor, and they stepped into the hallway. A man who had been standing in front of the door of their suite approached them.

He looked harmless enough, but she felt the muscles of Kyle's arm tense beneath her hand. The stranger, a pleasant-looking young man with short blond hair and fashionable glasses, extended his hand.

"I'm David Hall, the resident manager," he said. "Welcome to the Hilton, Mr. and Mrs. Foster."

Kyle relaxed and shook the manager's hand. "Thank you."

Mrs. Foster, she thought. *That would take some getting used to.*

Hall turned, led the way to the suite and threw open the door. "I hope we have everything you requested. If not, please let me know, and I'll take care of it personally."

"Thanks," Kyle said.

"Enjoy your stay." The manager sauntered toward the elevator.

Laura hurried into the suite. Kyle followed and closed the door.

He gave a low whistle of approval. "Not too shabby."

Laura surveyed the comfortable sitting room, decorated with several arrangements of fresh flowers. A basket of fruit, crackers and exotic cheeses graced the coffee table, and a magnum of champagne cooled beside it in a silver bucket filled with ice. Huge picture windows overlooked planes taking off and landing from the nearby airport, but the thick walls of the hotel muffled their noise.

Kyle peeled off his suit jacket, removed his tie and rolled up the sleeves of his dress shirt. "Might as well make yourself comfortable."

Suddenly overcome with self-consciousness, she removed the jacket of her dusky-rose silk dress, kicked off her matching shoes and curled into the corner of one of the deep sofas. If they'd been truly newlyweds, what to do next wouldn't have been a problem, but now the long hours of the afternoon and evening stretched endlessly ahead of her.

With an expert twist, Kyle opened the champagne and poured her a glass.

"It's a good thing we have this time together." He handed her the filled flute.

"Why's that?" She took a wary sip of the cold bubbly. In her ambivalent state of mind, she'd have to be careful how much alcohol she consumed. She didn't want to succumb to her attraction to Kyle and make their circumstances any more tense than they already were.

He settled into the opposite corner of the sofa and propped his feet on the coffee table. "We need time to get our stories straight."

"About the wedding?"

"About everything."

The gravity in his voice and the grim set of his strong jaw reminded her of the seriousness of their sham wedding. They had married not for love, but to set a trap for the terrorists' contact in her father's lab.

"We have a lot to learn about each other," he said, "if we're going to convince folks we've been close for the past few years."

She tucked her stocking feet beneath her and took another fortifying gulp of her drink. He looked so solid, so enticingly masculine that the prospect of spending the afternoon sharing her most intimate secrets made her tingle—and not from the champagne. She was finding her new husband entirely too appealing. Keeping the conversation on an impersonal level would make her life a heck of a lot easier right now.

"I have a list of conferences and seminars in my luggage, places we could have met when other members of the Institute weren't around." She started to rise.

"Stay put. We'll hit the small stuff first."

"Small stuff?"

He threw his arm across the back of the sofa and shifted to face her. "Yeah, like the fact that I despise artichokes."

He seemed so comfortable and at ease she couldn't help relaxing herself. "Then we have something in common."

During the next hour, she learned that he liked his potatoes baked, his favorite dessert was butter-pecan ice cream and his favorite beer Red Dog. His preferred vacation spot was Jackson Hole, Wyoming. He recounted stories of growing up on the citrus groves with his mother and father, who still managed the family land nearby with the help of immigrant workers, from whom Kyle had learned to speak passable Spanish as a child. He'd gone on to study chemistry and biology in college.

Losing her self-consciousness, she confessed her love of pasta and her favorite dessert, tiramisu. New York City, she admitted, with its theaters, museums and shops, was her favorite getaway. She shared with him the loneliness of her childhood in Eastern boarding schools and the isolation of her high-school years spent in a Swiss finishing school where she learned fluent French, German and Italian.

Remembering her unhappiness as a child who spent so much time away from her father made her think of Kyle's little girl.

"What did you tell Molly about us?" she asked.

Kyle split the last of the champagne between their glasses and resumed his corner of the sofa. "This morning I told her I was going away for a day or two with Frank. Our work often requires that, so she didn't think anything was out of the ordinary."

"And when we go back?"

"I figured I'd take a couple days to settle in at the Institute before I bring Molly to live there."

"But you *are* going to tell her?"

"That we're married?" He stared into the distance, avoiding her eyes. "That's going to be a problem."

Laura felt a dull pain beneath her breastbone. "You think she won't like me?"

He shook his head. "I think she'll like you too much."

Pleasure cascaded through her at his claim. "And that's bad?"

"It will be when we've caught the mole in the lab, and Molly and I return to the Lonesome Pony. Although she's too young to remember much, Molly was deserted by her mother. I don't want her to feel deserted by you, too."

Laura chewed thoughtfully on her bottom lip. "You don't dare tell her that you'll only be at the Institute temporarily."

"Right. Molly's very open and talkative. Unless she believes we're truly married—and for the long haul, she might give our secret away."

The last thing Laura wanted was to upset the adorable Molly. "When the time comes, we can ease the transition. I can spend time with her at the ranch, so she doesn't feel abandoned."

The approval on his face warmed her as much as the champagne she'd consumed. "You'd do that?"

"Absolutely. In the past few weeks, I've learned what it's like to lose a parent. I wouldn't want Molly to suffer like I have."

"If you spend time with her later, when all this is over, I think she'll be okay. She's a pretty resilient kid. Took the move to Montana in stride."

Laura flashed him a smile. "With the help of a pony."

Kyle nodded. "Returning to Ribbons will be a consolation, too."

And how will I feel, Laura wondered, *when both Kyle and Molly walk out of my life for good? Will I be able to endure the loneliness again?*

"Hungry?" Kyle asked.

Shaken from her thoughts, Laura knew he was talking about ordering dinner, but her deepest hunger wasn't for food. Even though she was reluctant ever to marry again, to risk anew the hurt that Curt had inflicted on her, she longed for a family of her own. Josiah had been her only family for so long, and with him gone, she had never felt so alone.

Until she met Kyle Foster.

But her association with Kyle, no matter how intimate it appeared on the surface, was strictly temporary, and if she let herself feel otherwise, her former loneliness and isolation would only boomerang more intensely when he and Molly returned to their cabin at the ranch. Kyle was worried about breaking Molly's heart. For the sake of her own heart, Laura would have to keep her emotional distance from both Kyle and Molly.

She steeled herself against his charm. "Hungry? You're talking about our wedding supper?"

"If you don't mind room service."

"You order," she suggested. "Surprise me."

LATER, over coffee, however, she couldn't help delving deeper into what made her new husband tick. "Your degrees are in biology and chemistry. How did you end up in law enforcement?"

"Looking back, I was destined to end up in law enforcement, but it took a while for me to realize it."

"Something from your childhood?"

"Partly. When I was in elementary school, there was a boy in my class, a big kid with a low IQ who'd been held back a couple grades. He wasn't happy, and he did his best to make every other kid in school miserable, too. He extorted their lunch money by threatening to beat them up. And he could have, he was that huge.''

She tried to imagine Kyle as a youngster, with baby fat like Molly, and chubby arms and legs, but she couldn't get past the rugged, muscular *now* of him.

''He took my money one day,'' Kyle said, ''and I went home and told my father, hoping Dad would take care of him. But Dad insisted stopping him was up to me, that I should always stand up to bullies, who were basically cowards at heart.''

''So you fought him?''

Kyle laughed. ''No, thank God. That big gorilla would have mopped up the floor with me. I was just a skinny little kid. No, I did what Dad said and refused to hand over my lunch money the next time. And Dad was right. The bully was afraid to fight. The other kids witnessed my success, and from then on, the bully was out of business.''

''That's why you became a cop?''

''In a way, yes. I'd always loved science, and I was enjoying my work as a researcher after I graduated, but I missed working with people. Alone all day in the lab, I didn't have a chance to make many friends. My best friend was Ted, this old fellow who lived in the apartment next door to me. He'd hit the beach at Normandy on D day, survived the war in Europe, came home, raised a family and outlived them all. He was barely scratching by on his social security, but he was generous with me to a fault. He'd have me over for dinner often, and afterward he'd tell stories of World War II. He never bragged, but I could read through the lines. What his generation did for this country was extraordinary. It was a shame after giving so much, the old guy was living out his last days in near poverty.''

Caught up in the story, mesmerized by the passion shining in his green eyes, Laura shifted closer to Kyle.

"One evening after working late," he said, "I was walking home from the lab and spotted a crowd and several police cars and an ambulance near my building. When I approached, paramedics were lifting a shrouded body into the ambulance. Someone beside me muttered that an old man had been beaten to death.''

Tears glistened in Kyle's eyes, and with a sinking feeling in her stomach, Laura guessed where his story was heading.

"I found out the next morning that Ted was the man who died. Some punk had jumped him for the money from the social security check he'd just cashed. I remembered the tough kid from my school days, and my father's insistence that I had to stand up against bullies. After Ted died, I couldn't return to the safety and isolation of the laboratory, not while scum roamed the streets preying on innocent people like that sweet old man. I quit my job and enrolled in the next session at the police academy.''

"Any regrets?"

His eyes clouded with an even deeper pain. "Oh, yeah."

For several long minutes, he was quiet. She'd treaded on dangerous ground with her question, from the look of him, and she didn't know if she wanted him to explain or move on.

He lifted his head with a shake, as if waking from a bad dream. "I wish I'd never joined the bomb squad."

"What?" She hadn't known.

"For the first few years, I was a street cop, working to keep the Teds of the world safe. Then my chief discovered my chemistry background and persuaded me to join the bomb squad."

"Working on bombs—wasn't it terrifying?"

"God, yes. Everyone in the demolition unit was scared sh...senseless. It went with the territory. But that's not the cause of my regrets."

She sat still, waiting, watching the pain flit across his face. If he wanted to tell her, she'd listen. If not, she wouldn't push him.

"If I hadn't joined the squad," he said, "maybe Buzz Williams, my former partner, would still be alive."

As if exorcising a horrible ghost, he told her the entire story of the bomb at the Hollywood Bowl, Buzz's insistence on defusing it, and the subsequent explosion. She understood now where the scar across his eyebrow originated.

"You shouldn't blame yourself," she insisted. "Buzz was doing what he wanted to do. He knew the risks, just as you did."

"Have you been talking to the LAPD shrink?" he asked with a twisted grin. "You're singing the same tune."

She moved away from the painful subject. "You said you quit after Buzz died. Why did you join Montana Confidential?"

"Because Daniel persuaded me."

"How?"

Anger and determination turned his eyes to green fire. "He told me we'd be going after terrorists. And terrorists, especially ones with bombs and biological weapons, are the biggest bullies of all."

Chapter Seven

Kyle stifled a yawn, leaned back against the jet's cushioned seat and closed his eyes. He hadn't slept much the night before, but not for the usual honeymoon reasons. He and Laura had talked until almost 2:00 a.m., getting the story of their fake courtship, engagement and marriage straight for the staff at the Quinlan Research Institute.

She had given him detailed descriptions of the members of the staff, starting with Dr. Lawrence Tyson, the head researcher, all the way down to Wayne Pritchard, a research assistant. Any one of them could be the Institute's inside connection to the Black Order, but from the background Laura gave him, Kyle had no idea where to cast suspicion. He'd have to keep his eyes and ears open and hope the traitor would make a mistake that pointed to his or her identity.

In the intimate luxury of the honeymoon suite, he and Laura had shared every fact about each other that might present a stumbling block in their deception; every fact, that is, except the details of their divorces. Laura's emotions were still obviously raw from the

loss of her father, and Kyle hadn't wanted to cause
more pain with questions about a subject she clearly
intended to avoid. As for himself, his feelings for
Alicia had withered and died long before she left
him, so talking about her wasn't that painful. It just
didn't seem relevant. He'd told Laura only that his
ex-wife had remarried, then changed the subject, not
wanting her to feel the obligation of an informational
quid pro quo.

He lay wide-eyed for hours fixing the names and
information about the Institute staff in his mind, but
even if he hadn't had that mental exercise to keep
him awake, he doubted he'd have slept much. The
daring and risk of their deception weighed on him.
He'd have to remain alert, both mentally and physi-
cally, at the Institute. Otherwise, he'd be putting not
only himself but Laura and Molly in danger if he
made a slip.

Despite his fatigue, once Kyle had cleared his
mind of the upcoming mission, he'd still found sleep
elusive. Laura had left the door to the bedroom open,
in case he needed to use the bathroom during the
night. From the sofa where he slept in the suite's
sitting room, he could hear the slight rustle of the
sheets as she turned in her sleep and the faint whisper
of her regular breathing.

Kyle had expected their marriage-in-name-only
ploy to be a tricky situation, strewn with as much
potential for disaster as a Bosnian minefield. What
he hadn't expected was his inability to tame his rebellious emotions. When the fusty little judge who
stank of cigar smoke had declared them husband and

wife and directed Kyle to kiss his bride, he'd been overcome with the desire to sweep her into his arms and kiss her senseless. The intensity of his desire had shaken him, and he'd needed every shred of discipline and self-control he could muster to keep his kiss impersonal. In the few hours that had remained until dawn, he'd tossed and turned on the sofa, wondering how he'd manage to keep his emotional distance while providing a display of affection convincing enough for the Institute staff to believe he and Laura were true newlyweds.

The soft touch of her hand on his arm pulled him from his thoughts. "We're almost there."

He opened his eyes to the sweet smile lighting her periwinkle blue eyes and turning up the corners of her delectable mouth and groaned inwardly.

What had he gotten himself into?

Her smile vanished, and he realized his expression must have reflected his thoughts.

"You okay?" Her soft voice was filled with concern.

He didn't have to force a smile in return. Just being close to her made him want to grin like an idiot. "Fine," he answered. "Or at least, nothing wrong that a good night's sleep wouldn't cure."

C.J. giggled in the seat ahead of him, leaned into the aisle, and glanced back at them with a smug look on her pretty face. "That's the way I like to hear honeymooners talk."

Before Kyle could issue an appropriate comeback, the jet touched down on the tarmac at the Bozeman airport, and they were unbuckling seatbelts, gathering overnight bags and disembarking the plane.

Frank, his arm around C.J., stopped on the runway and turned to Kyle. "C.J. and I will take care of the paperwork in the airport office, then I'll drive her back to the Institute."

Kyle nodded. "We have the Quinlan SUV. Laura and I will stop by the ranch first to see Molly, then head for—"

"Home," Laura said. "I want Kyle to see the layout of the Institute before dark."

Kyle shook Frank's hand and thanked him for his help, while C.J. hugged Laura and whispered a long time in her ear. Laura answered her too softly for Kyle to hear, and C.J. turned away laughing. Then the newlyweds headed for the parking lot.

"What was that all about?" Kyle asked.

"What?"

"C.J.'s whispers."

Her eyes glinted with mischief. "You don't want to know."

"I have to know," he insisted. "We can't have secrets if our masquerade is going to work."

Laura sighed. "Well, if you must know, she said you're a stunningly attractive man, and it's too damn bad we didn't have a real wedding night."

Kyle felt his face redden in spite of his efforts to remain unperturbed. "What did you tell her?"

Laura's demeanor was stern. "That if she made a move on my new husband, I'd scratch her eyes out." A muscle tugged at the side of her mouth as she apparently struggled to keep a serious face.

Surprised by her feisty retort, Kyle burst out laughing, and Laura joined in. The tension he'd felt earlier dissolved. "As long as we can keep our sense of humor, Mrs. Foster, this fake marriage of ours will be a piece of cake."

Their levity, however, was short-lived. On the drive back to Lonesome Pony, Kyle had Laura grill him on the information she'd given him about the Institute and the staff. In spite of their joking at the airport, they both were well aware of the gravity of their situation.

Daniel came out to greet them when they arrived at the ranch.

"I've contacted the security company in Billings," he said quietly, after a round of boisterous congratulations that rang across the yard, loud enough for any ranch hand within shouting distance to hear. "Monty Slater, the owner, will pay you a visit at the Institute tomorrow. He's a good man, retired FBI. You can trust him with your life."

A high-pitched squeal sounded from near the barn, and Kyle glanced up to see Molly barreling down the driveway as fast as her chubby legs would carry her.

"Daddy! Daddy! You're back!"

He swept his daughter into his arms and hugged her tight. She lifted her head and glanced shyly at Laura. "Hello, Miss Laura."

Laura reached over and tousled Molly's curls. "Hi, sweetheart."

The warmth of Molly's reciprocating smile left little doubt how fond Molly was of Laura.

"I'm back, doodlebug," Kyle said, "but only for

a little while. I have to leave again in a few minutes. I just came by to say hello to my favorite girl.''

''Mrs. McMurty?'' Devilment shone in Molly's eyes.

''Why, yes,'' Kyle answered, pretending surprise. ''How did you guess?''

''Oh, Daddy!'' She smacked him on the shoulder with her tiny fist. ''You know *I'm* you're favorite girl.''

''You sure are.'' His heart ached with love for the child. He hated being away from her and was sorry to have to leave again so quickly. ''I have to go away for a couple days, but I'll be back soon, and I'll call you every night.''

''You going with Frank and Court and Daniel?''

''Not this time. I'm going with Miss Laura.''

''I like Miss Laura. Can I go, too?''

Laura caressed the little girl's cheek. ''Not this time, but the next time. I promise.''

''Molly!'' Jewel's impatient shout emanated above them from the corral. ''You gonna ride this pony or not?''

Molly wriggled in his arms, and Kyle set her on her feet. ''Gotta go, Daddy. Jewel's waiting.''

He bent and kissed her again before she rocketed toward the barn.

Daniel grinned. ''No need to worry about her. She's happy as a pig in mud, and Dale and Jewel keep a close eye on her.''

''I'm glad it'll only be a few more days.'' Kyle's impatience bubbled to a boiling point. ''This whole process is taking too long. The Black Order could be back in Agar now, for all we know.''

Daniel's brown eyes glowed with understanding. ''We're all in a hurry to catch those bastards, but taking the time to establish your cover is crucial. If you're not believable as Laura's husband and the new administrator of the Institute, we could lose you and let the terrorists slip away and take the D-5 with them. Slow and steady. That's the only way to pull this off.''

Kyle jammed his hands in the pockets of his jacket and flashed his boss a rueful grin. ''You're right, of course.''

''Dale packed your things this morning. You can load them while Jewel keeps Molly busy.''

Laura glanced anxiously toward the little girl, treading toward the barn. ''Won't Molly worry when she sees Kyle's clothes missing?''

Daniel shook his head. ''She's staying in the main house in Jewel's room, so she won't notice. Dale will have Molly's things packed up, too, by the time you come back for her. Sure you don't want to tell Molly about the move now?''

Kyle shook his head. ''She might fret about it without me here to reassure her.''

He kept to himself the fact that he wasn't moving Molly to the Institute until he'd checked it out himself and was convinced his daughter would be safe there.

LAURA WAITED in the vehicle while Patrick McMurty helped Kyle shift his suitcases from the cabin into the SUV. She'd seen the pain that clouded Kyle's eyes when he'd said goodbye to Molly. The man was a paradox. Tough as nails on the outside, with the iron nerves to face down fanatical terrorists or disarm destructive devices, but held inside all a father's love and tenderness toward his daughter that were a joy to behold.

With Kyle's clothes stowed aboard, he slammed the gate of the SUV with a solid *thunk,* thanked Patrick with a handshake and climbed into the driver's seat. He started the car and headed down the driveway. From the corral, Molly, atop Ribbons, waved happily. Kyle blew her a kiss and continued past the main house toward the highway. From the look on his face, Laura could tell he was missing Molly already.

For the next half hour, they traveled in companionable silence, as if both were all talked out from their overnight information marathon, but as they neared the turnoff to the Institute, Kyle glanced across at her.

"Nervous?" he asked.

She shook her head. "I'll be on home turf. You're the one who has to deal with unknown territory and strangers."

"You've prepared me well."

His praise pleased her. "You think so?"

He reached across the well between the seats, took her hand and squeezed it gently. "Things have happened so fast, I haven't had time to tell you I think you're a pretty special lady. Your father would be proud."

At the mention of her dad, her ever-present grief surfaced, and she brushed away a tear. She had to concentrate on avenging her father and not let her sadness overwhelm her. "That's the whole point of all this, to catch Daddy's killers. I've never favored the death penalty before, but now I'm ready to make an exception. I'll do whatever it takes to bring these terrorists to justice."

"Like marrying a total stranger?" Kyle's sunny grin eased her sorrow. "You've got spunk."

"You call it spunk. I call it crazy, but I guess I've been crazy since Daddy died. Having my world turned upside down was enough to drive me over the edge."

"You're one of the sanest people I've ever met. Otherwise, I'd never have agreed to this scheme. I've put my life in your hands."

Admiration was evident in the expression on his handsome face. She stared into eyes like a green ocean, deep enough to drown in, then yanked her glance away. She liked Kyle Foster. Too much. If she didn't maintain her detachment, she'd find herself as heartbroken when he finished his assignment, annulled their marriage and left her as she had been when Curt deceived her. She didn't need more heartache, so she tamped down her emotions and changed the direction of the conversation.

"You've never been to the Institute?"

"Flew over it once in the ranch chopper, but not close enough to see it clearly."

They had followed the turnoff to the entrance to the blind canyon where her father had built the facility of his dreams. Ten-foot chain-link fencing topped with razor wire stretched across the mouth of the canyon, a gate with a guardhouse the only entrance. Kyle slowed the car as they approached, and the gate swung open with an electronic hum. A guard waved them through.

Kyle scowled and bit back a curse.

"What's wrong?"

He jerked his head back toward the entrance as the SUV passed unchallenged through the gate. "That's something that will have to change. I'll speak to Monty Slater about it tomorrow."

"The gate?" she asked.

"Not the gate. The guard. First, he didn't make us stop to show identification. Anyone could have been driving this car. He shouldn't have opened the gate until he was certain who we were. Second, he wasn't armed. And third, even if he had been armed, he shouldn't be alone. It's too easy to overwhelm one person. The Black Order could bring a caravan through that gate and meet no resistance."

Laura shivered. She hadn't realized how inadequate the Institute's security was. By the time Kyle and Monty Slater, the security specialist, finished their inspection tomorrow, she was certain they'd find other weaknesses in the facility's protection.

"Stop here," she told him. "It's the best view."

Kyle had slowed the SUV when he entered the gate, and now he braked at the lip of the canyon before the road dipped to the valley floor. Ahead, the road forked. To the left, the road traveled up along the side of the canyon wall to the director's house.

She looked at her home where she'd lived for the past year and tried to see it through Kyle's eyes, as if for the first time.

With its gleaming expanse of windows that soared two stories high, its solid log walls and wide welcoming porches and balconies with terrific vistas, it resembled an expensive hunting lodge. Behind it, the canyon wall had been excavated to provide a large, level lawn that surrounded the house.

"That's it." She pointed to the house. "Home, sweet home."

Kyle gave a whistle of appreciation. "That's a big place. The three of us could get lost in there."

"Daddy wanted room to entertain the staff, but not all the rooms are huge."

"And the bedrooms?"

His tone was neutral, but the topic of his question made her pulse race. "Five, more than enough for all of us."

"That's going to be a problem."

"I don't see why. We each have our own room—"

"And if someone's suspicious and keeping an eye on the house, they'll be watching the lights go on and off, checking which rooms are being used. We're supposed to be newlyweds, remember?"

This was a problem she intended to nip in the bud. "Then I guess you'll have to get used to dressing and undressing in the dark."

Kyle laughed. "You have an answer for everything, don't you?"

She grinned back at him, glad the tense moment had passed. "I try."

She pointed past the main house where the road snaked through a copse of fir trees. At the far edge of the forested area, a series of condominiums, smaller but in an architectural style that matched the main house, seemed to hang perilously from the canyon wall. "Staff housing."

"Looks like vacation hideaways."

"Daddy wanted the staff and their families to be comfortable, especially since we're out here in the middle of nowhere."

"Speaking of nowhere—" Kyle's glance swept the valley floor "—where's the lab?"

"Take the right fork into the valley."

Kyle eased the car down the steep road and circled a high grassy hill that rose from the canyon floor.

"Stop here," she directed.

He braked and gazed around him at the grass-covered hillock and bare canyon walls. "What am I supposed to be looking at?"

She grinned, pleased at the deception. "The laboratory."

"Right. Your father was not only a microbiologist but a magician. His lab's invisible."

"That's right. It *is* invisible." She stifled a laugh at his perplexed expression. "Drive ahead, just around that curve. Then stop again."

Kyle did as she instructed. Around the curve, he halted the car once more and glanced to his left.

"Wow."

He exhaled the exclamation as if someone had

punched him in the stomach, delighting Laura with his response.

"See, I told you it was invisible—at least everywhere but here."

"It's underground!"

"Except for this side. The three-story glass facade provides light and solar heating. With the rest of the building built into the hill, we take advantage of geothermal heating and cooling. Keeps the electric bills down." Her smile faded as she remembered the other reason for the design. "Having the lab underground also provides easier containment if we ever have an accident."

"That's a scary thought," Kyle said.

She nodded in agreement. "There's a built-in alarm system with panic buttons in every room. If there's a spill or contamination of any kind, someone hits the alarm, a siren sounds, and huge shutters with impermeable membranes close over the entire facade. If we move fast enough, nothing harmful escapes into the atmosphere."

"What about the people inside?"

"There are various safe areas throughout the building, but everyone would most likely don hazard suits and start the cleanup."

"Let's hope that never happens."

Laura nodded in agreement. "When you're dealing with deadly viruses and bacteria, you learn to be careful. Want to see inside?"

"Not yet. I'd rather greet all the staff at once at the meeting you've called for tomorrow morning."

The late-afternoon sun, about to disappear over the

rim of the canyon wall, glinted off the lab's high windows. Kyle started the car again and continued up the road, which looped past the staff condos and eventually led to the director's house. He pulled into the circular driveway and stopped by the front steps. With the boundless energy that never ceased to amaze her, he hopped from the car, circled it and opened the door for her. Together they climbed the broad front stairs, and Laura fumbled in her purse for her key.

While she was trying to locate it, Kyle suddenly grabbed her, pulled her close, and before she could utter a protest, pressed his mouth to hers. She started to resist, but he quickly moved to nibble at her ear and whispered, "Play along with me. We're being watched."

Participating in his kiss didn't prove a hardship. Although her mind still reeled from surprise, her body responded readily to the warmth of his embrace, and she relaxed in his arms, lifting her lips for another kiss, savoring the honeyed taste of him, reveling in the aromas of sunshine, soap and leather, and his distinctively masculine scent. Because he was only a few inches taller, she had merely to stand on tiptoe for their bodies to meld into a perfect fit. She wrapped her arms around him and flexed her fingers over the taut muscles of his back.

Excitement thrummed along her nerves, underlaid by a more powerful feeling. In Kyle's arms, she felt safe again for the first time since her father died.

Kyle pulled away and graced her with a grin so

ridiculously lopsided and enchantingly appealing that her stomach somersaulted.

"The key?" he said.

Still intoxicated from the force of his kiss, she couldn't make sense of his request. "What?"

"I have to unlock the door if we're going to do this right."

Blushing at her awkwardness, she reached into her purse, found the key and handed it to him. With a quick flick of his wrist, he unlocked the door, thrust the key in his pocket, then scooped her into his arms as if she weighed no more than a blade of grass.

"Smile, Mrs. Foster," he muttered under his breath. "You're supposed to be enjoying this."

Shaking away her bewilderment, Laura threw her arms around his neck and assumed a radiant expression. Playacting wasn't hard. She *felt* radiant in Kyle's arms, swept over the threshold in his strong arms like a real bride.

Once inside, Kyle kicked the door shut and set her on her feet. "That was close," he said. "If I hadn't caught a glimpse of someone watching from the trees, we might have blown our whole cover."

"Who was it? What did he look like?"

Kyle shook his head. "Couldn't tell. Don't even know if the person was male or female. Whoever it was was making an effort *not* to be seen, but he was still watching as we came through the door."

A shiver rippled down Laura's spine before her common sense kicked in. "It could have been entirely innocent. One of the staff out for a walk and curious to see what I'm up to."

"Maybe. Anyone here know about the wedding?"

"Only C.J."

"Good. I know she's kept our secret. Tomorrow I can gauge reactions in the staff meeting when you announce our marriage. It'll be interesting to note who *isn't* surprised."

Still feeling chilled, she crossed the room to the thermostat on the far wall and turned up the heat. The furnace kicked in with a faint whisper of moving air, and a current of warmth eddied about the room. "I still find it hard to believe we have a traitor on staff. I know them. They're all good people."

Kyle's appealing grin had disappeared, his face now set in grim lines. "Even good people have their breaking points. Some even have a price. You have to remember, you can't trust anyone but C.J."

"And you."

His smile returned. "If you can't trust your own husband, who can you trust?" He headed for the door. "I'll bring in the luggage and see if I can sneak another look at our resident snoop."

Before opening the door, he turned back. "This house have an alarm system?"

Laura shook her head. "Daddy never thought we needed one."

Kyle grimaced. "I'll add that to the list for Monty Slater tomorrow."

A few minutes later he manhandled the luggage into the foyer. "Lead the way."

Laura preceded him up the stairs and stopped at the first door. "This is my old room. It has twin beds, so you can sleep here and keep Molly with you until she becomes accustomed to the house.''

Kyle merely nodded, but kept hold of the suitcases. ''And your room?''

She continued down the hall. ''Right next door.''

Stepping into the spacious master bedroom that had once been her father's, she was confronted immediately by the immense king-size bed that faced soaring windows that overlooked the forest, and felt a fleeting moment of regret that her marriage to Kyle wasn't real, that he wouldn't be sharing her bed that night. Then she thrust the enticing notion aside.

Kyle deposited all the suitcases on the bed, then opened his and began hanging his clothes beside hers in the immense walk-in closet.

''Wait.'' The command came out more strident and high-pitched than she'd intended.

Clothes in one hand, hangers in the other, Kyle turned at her order and contemplated her with a raised eyebrow, his left one bisected by the fascinating crescent scar.

Feeling flustered and embarrassed—and angry at him for putting her in such a position, she lifted her chin and met his green gaze with an unflinching stare. ''We agreed you'd sleep in the other room.''

''That's right,'' he said in an agreeable tone before returning to the closet. When he'd finished hanging up his clothes, he removed his shaving kit and stepped around her where she stood like a sentinel in the middle of the room. He entered the master bath and unpacked his toiletries, lining them neatly on the marble countertop.

Shaking her head in confusion, she followed him into the bathroom. "If you're sleeping in the other room, why are you unpacking in here?"

He grasped her gently by the shoulders and gazed into her eyes. "I know this is hard for you, and I promise not to intrude on your privacy any more than necessary. I can sleep next door, but my clothes and personal belongings have to remain in this room."

"Why?" His closeness, the touch of his hands on her shoulders and the gentle understanding in his voice were making her giddy. "No one comes in here but me."

"I hope you're right. But if anyone should become suspicious and arrange to search the house, we don't want to give ourselves away by obviously occupying separate rooms."

Realizing his reasoning, she felt foolish, having assumed he'd been pushing himself on her by moving into her room. From the little she'd learned about Kyle Foster, she should have known better. He had a rare quality not often found in today's world: he was a consummate gentleman.

Later, however, after a quick supper of soup and sandwiches when Kyle had sequestered himself in her father's office with the personnel files, Laura sat alone before a roaring fire in the family room and sipped a cup of herbal tea. Experiencing an irrational pang of disappointment that Kyle wouldn't be sharing her room and her bed, she convinced herself her feelings were strictly the result of fear. With an unknown traitor in their midst, she felt safer the closer she was to Kyle.

She viewed him merely as a protector, she assured herself. After what Curt had done to her heart, she doubted she'd ever fall in love again.

THE NEXT MORNING, Kyle stood in the rear of the laboratory's conference room and observed the various members of the staff as they filed in and took seats around the table for the specially called meeting. He'd spent hours the night before memorizing personnel records, placing photographed faces to names and faxing data to Court at the ranch so that he could run background and credit checks on everyone.

Keeping busy had *almost* helped him forget he shared a house, particularly a closet and a bathroom, with a woman who made his pulse race. Luckily, by closeting himself in Josiah's study, he'd placed enough distance between him and Laura to be able to concentrate. That is, until she knocked on the door at ten o'clock and entered wearing a frilly robe and a sympathetic, blue-eyed smile, and carrying a tray filled with cinnamon-laced hot chocolate and homemade cookies. If the way to a man's heart was through his stomach, Laura had the route clearly marked. He'd shooed her away quickly before he'd been tempted to play newlyweds again. Unlike the previous afternoon, he'd have had a hard time claiming bystanders were watching in the middle of the Quinlan home.

Jerking his thoughts back to the present and his assignment, he silently delivered himself a stern lecture on the dangers of pretty distractions like Laura

Quinlan. He had a traitor to catch, an apparently wily and creative informer who'd managed to operate in the intimate surroundings of the lab with a staff that was more like family, and yet had managed to fool them all.

Kyle surveyed the room as he waited. In such pleasant surroundings he found it hard to believe that evil such as the Black Order could exist, even though his memories of the capitol bombing told him otherwise. On the third floor of the laboratory building, the floor-to-ceiling glass wall of the conference room offered a breathtaking view of the mountain ranges in their fall splendor. High above a nearby peak already crusted with early snow, a bald eagle circled, riding on the currents of a chinook wind that warmed the autumn day. Inside, an oblong table of light wood with matching chairs in a Scandinavian design were the only objects of furniture in the room.

Kyle watched Dr. Lawrence Tyson enter first. Tall and rangy in his immaculately pressed lab coat, the scientist's craggy, wrinkled face and thick gray hair made him appear older than his fifty-two years. With a murmur of greeting to Laura, he took his place beside her at the head of the table, plopped a yellow legal pad in front of him and commenced doodling with a Mont Blanc pen while waiting for the others.

C.J. came next, accompanied by Dr. Melinda Kwan, the only other female on the staff. An attractive Asian-American with smooth, sculpted features and thick black hair cut blunt above her shoulders, Dr. Kwan cast a curious look at Kyle before seating herself at the foot of the table, as far as she could

get from Dr. Tyson. Once her fleeting glance of in-
quisitiveness had disappeared, she assumed an impassive expression that Kyle found impossible to
read.

Interesting, he thought, and wondered if distancing
herself from the head researcher indicated animosity
toward her colleague or simply a desire to sit near
the door for a quick getaway once the meeting ended.

From the other end of the room, Laura caught
Kyle's eye and smiled, and for an instant the sweetness of her expression drove his entire mission from
his mind. Keeping up their just-married appearances,
he returned her look with a warm grin, then forced
himself to turn back toward the door to scrutinize the
latest arrival.

Judging from the red hair and freckled counte-
nance of the young man who'd just entered, Kyle
pegged him as Gary Bowen, a research assistant in
his twenties who worked primarily with Dr. Tyson.
Bowen slid awkwardly into a chair next to his boss
and sat clicking and retracting the nib on a ballpoint
pen and shifting constantly in his chair, a perfect
poster boy for hyperactivity.

Following close on Bowen's heels was Dr. Robert
Potter, a rotund, balding little man in his forties, second in command to Tyson, according to the notes in
Josiah Quinlan's desk. Potter seemed to bounce on
the balls of his feet, his smile was one-hundred-watt
and his cheery, ''Good morning, all,'' reverberated
through the room. He took a seat next to C.J. and
surveyed his fellow staff members with what appeared to be eager expectation.

Wayne Pritchard, the other research assistant, who floated his duties between the remaining four scientists, sauntered into the conference room last. Kyle didn't regard himself as a judge of masculine pulchritude, but he figured Pritchard, with his symmetrical, well-shaped features, tall, athletic build and thick, dark hair above keen brown eyes would be considered handsome by most women. With a nod to the others in the room and a murmured, "Sorry, I'm late," Pritchard hurried to his place.

As soon as Pritchard had folded his long legs into the chair on the other side of Bowen, Kyle moved to the front of the room and sat at Laura's left. Kyle had known better than to hope one of the staff would have sported a guilty expression that gave him away, but he was disappointed that his usually sensitive radar, a very dependable intuition, hadn't sent him any signals about who the terrorist informant in the group might be.

Laura stood and addressed the group. "Good morning, everyone, and thank you for coming on such short notice. I'll try not to keep you from your work any longer than necessary."

Kyle felt a rush of pride. Any man would be proud to call Laura Quinlan wife. Even in casual navy wool slacks and a muted plaid blouse, she looked fashionably elegant. Wings of dark, thick hair swept her temples, and her eyes, as deep and blue as the October sky, sparkled.

"First," she continued, "I want to thank you again for the kindness you've shown me since my father died. You've been my family and seen me through the darkest time of my life. Words are inadequate to express how much I appreciate your support.''

While she spoke, Kyle scanned the faces of the people gathered around the table, ready for the slightest nuance of expression that might give away a traitor.

''You've carried on your work unfailingly in these hard times,'' Laura was saying, ''and I know Daddy would be proud of your dedication and professionalism.''

''You've done your fair share, too, Laura.'' Dr. Potter's round face beamed like a proud papa's. ''In spite of your difficult circumstances.''

''Thank you.'' With an attractive blush staining her high cheekbones, she acknowledged his compliment with a gracious nod. ''And that brings me to the real reason for this morning's meeting.''

Tyson, Potter and Bowen leaned forward in their chairs in anticipation of her announcement. Kwan, Kyle noted, hadn't moved, and Pritchard looked bored. C.J., like Kyle, was watching their reactions.

Laura took a deep breath and gestured toward Kyle. ''I want to introduce my husband, Dr. Kyle Foster.''

''Husband!'' Dr. Tyson sputtered as if she'd blasphemed. ''You're married?''

Kyle's focused gaze swept the room. Potter's smile grew even broader, Kwan's attractive Asian features remained impassive and Bowen grinned and continued to clean his fingernails with a penknife. Emotion flashed briefly across Wayne Pritchard's handsome features, too quickly for Kyle to identify it, but he thought it might be jealousy. Not that he blamed the man. Laura Quinlan was a gorgeous woman.

"Kyle and I were married day before yesterday in Los Angeles." Laura was playing her role as new bride so flawlessly, Kyle found himself believing her. "We'd planned a wedding for next spring, but after Daddy died, we decided to marry right away so I wouldn't be alone here."

Scowling, Tyson slumped in his chair.

Potter rose to the occasion, his pleasant grin a happy counterpoint to Tyson's disapproval. "Congratulations and best wishes to you both. We all, I'm sure—" he fixed his stare on Tyson "—wish you much happiness."

He resumed his seat amid murmurs of congratulations from the others. Even Tyson managed to mutter, "Best wishes," but in a begrudging tone.

"But that's not all my news," Laura continued. "As you know, Daddy administered the Institute as well as working as a researcher. I've asked Kyle to step into Daddy's shoes, both to run the business end of our endeavors and to help with exploration of new antidotes and vaccines."

"What?" Tyson was on his feet, towering over Laura, his face livid, the veins bulging in his neck. Even the most casual observer could tell the scientist struggled to maintain his composure. "That's impossible."

Kyle was ready to leap to Laura's defense, but she remained unperturbed. With admirable poise, she faced Dr. Tyson. "Impossible, Lawrence? Why would you say such a thing?"

Tyson glared past her to Kyle with a look that could kill. "Because the man's a fraud."

Chapter Eight

Kyle exerted every ounce of physical self-control not to respond to Tyson's verbal bullying, while his mind struggled with the scientist's accusation.

Fraud?

What did Tyson know? Was he going to blow Kyle's cover before the operation even started? As much as he was torn between wanting to punch the pugnacious old geezer between the eyes or to demand what he meant by charges of fraud, Kyle sat, outwardly calm, knowing that Laura, with her long-time association with Tyson, was best able to defuse the situation.

She flashed Tyson a tight smile. "I'm trying very hard not to take offense at the insult you've just flung at my husband, Lawrence, and to attribute your lack of courtesy to the fact that you're overworked—and stressed out by Daddy's death. I know he was your best friend."

The fight seemed to leak out of Tyson like air from a punctured balloon. He slumped back into his chair. "You're right. Forgive me, Laura. You took me by surprise."

"It's okay." Her voice was gentle, and she placed her hand on his shoulder in a comforting gesture. "I understand."

Tyson made a visible effort to pull himself together. He pushed to his feet, approached Kyle and extended his hand. "My apologies to you, too, Dr. Foster."

Kyle grasped the man's hard, bony hand. "Call me Kyle. No offense taken."

Tyson returned to his seat, and at the other end of the table, Melinda Kwan, her face as inscrutable as ever, spoke for the first time. "Meaning no disrespect, Laura, but you know how dangerous our work is here. For all our sakes, I'd like to know what Dr. Tyson meant when he called your husband a fraud."

Tyson had the grace to look embarrassed. "All I meant was that I've never heard Dr. Foster's name mentioned in our line of work. I've never seen him published or heard him speak at a conference. He's an unknown as far as I'm concerned."

Kwan looked at Laura. "Dr. Tyson has a point."

Laura turned to Kyle, her face calm but with a hint of panic in her eyes. "Maybe you'd better respond."

Kyle rose slowly to his feet. "Dr. Tyson's right, although I wouldn't call myself a fraud. My degrees and credentials are as valid as anyone's in this room. I don't, however, have as much experience as most of you in this field, nor am I as well known. That's one reason Laura and I felt the bulk of my time will be better spent in administration, to free the rest of you for the work you're so good at."

"Sounds reasonable to me." Dr. Potter nodded

with approval. The others' expressions remained neutral.

"I'll be meeting with each of you individually," Kyle said, "both to get to know you better and to learn your views on how the Institute should function. I'm here to help you not compete with you." He took his seat.

"I won't keep you from your work any longer," Laura said, "but before you go, I want to invite you and your families to a party at our house tomorrow night to help us celebrate."

After the staff dispersed, Kyle walked with Laura back to the house. He grasped her hand, intending to maintain their romantic charade, but he found himself enjoying the warmth of her hand in his and savoring the intimacy that small contact gave their stroll in the bright October sunshine.

"You didn't tell them about beefing up security," Laura said.

Kyle shook his head. "They'll find out soon enough. I don't want to alert the informer in case the Black Order has plans to steal anything else from the lab. Let's put the extra protection in place first."

She squeezed his hand, then halted her steps and turned to him, a softness in her expression that made his knees weak. "I can't thank you enough for being here. I don't know what I would have done without you."

He started to say he was just doing his job, but the sight of her checked his words. Through the quivering leaves of golden aspens that lined the road, the sun danced across her face, lighting her bright blue eyes and giving her silken skin an ethereal glow. Her rosy lips parted in a smile over perfect teeth, and the gentle breeze stirred her vibrant ebony hair, exposing her high, smooth forehead.

Without thinking, he placed his hands on her shoulders and pulled her toward him, claiming her lips with his own. Her unique orange-blossom scent swirled around him on the autumn air, firing his senses. He tugged her closer, and she came to him without resistance, draping her arms around his neck, molding her body to his. Even through the thickness of his denim jacket and chambray shirt, he felt the softness of her breasts against his chest and the thunderous beating of her heart.

He wanted to stand there forever with her in his arms, but his training kicked in, reminding him of his duty. If he didn't establish some emotional distance, he would be placing them both in danger. Reluctantly he pulled away.

The sweetness of her smile almost banished his resolve.

"I take it we were being watched again?" Her voice had a breathy quality, as if she couldn't get enough air.

Struggling for oxygen himself, he glanced back toward the glass facade of the Institute. "I thought I saw someone," he lied, "but whoever it was is gone now."

He couldn't let Laura know he was attracted to her. Although, on the one hand, he hoped, even suspected, she might welcome the idea, he had a double reason for maintaining his objectivity. First and fore-

most was his need to stay focused on his mission.
But he also realized how emotionally vulnerable she
was, having recently lost her father in such a violent
and tragic way. Even if he was free to give rein to
his growing affection for her, she deserved time to
grieve and heal without other encumbrances.

"You're getting pretty good at this playacting,"
he said with a lightness he hoped would convey he
hadn't taken their kiss seriously.

Her eyes darkened briefly, as if shrouded by a
passing shadow, then she laughed. "I'll race you
back to the house. Last one there has to fix lunch."

He permitted her a head start, not out of chivalry
but to allow himself the pleasure of watching her
long legs and slender hips glide up the road ahead
of him. When she rounded a curve and disappeared,
he took off running in earnest.

SINCE THEIR FOOTRACE had ended in a dead heat,
Laura grilled cheese sandwiches while Kyle heated
soup. She liked the way they worked together in the
kitchen. Curt had never helped with meals, claiming
them "women's work," but Kyle's familiarity with
utensils did nothing to diminish his masculinity.

If anything, his willingness to pitch in made him
even more attractive. And even more of a problem.
When Laura had concocted this marriage scheme,
she'd believed herself invulnerable to Kyle Foster's
magnetism, believed the pain Curt had caused her
would shield her from attraction to the handsome
cowboy. She hadn't counted on being knocked off
her feet by his kisses. Earlier on the road to the lab,

she'd been disappointed when Kyle had pulled away. She'd wanted the kiss to go on forever.

She chalked up her fascination with her new husband to stress and the emotional imbalance of grief, and tried to push it from her thoughts, reminding herself they had an informant to catch.

"Now that you've met the staff—" she turned the sandwiches on the griddle "—what are your impressions?"

Kyle straddled a tall stool by the counter and kept an eye on the simmering soup. "Dr. Tyson doesn't like me and makes no effort to hide it."

"At least that gives him honesty in his favor."

"I studied his file last night. Do you know his wife is Lebanese?"

"Zahra? I'd forgotten." Laura pictured the plump, smiling woman, her dark hair shot with gray. "She's been in this country since she was a little girl, so she seems totally American. She doesn't even speak with an accent."

"Does she have relatives in the Middle East?"

The intense expression on Kyle's face chilled her. She was glad she had nothing to hide from this man, who looked as if he'd spend his last breath to find the traitor. "I don't know, but I know neither she nor Lawrence would ever jeopardize the Institute."

"Even if the Black Order threatened her family?"

Laura shifted the sandwiches to plates, sliced them into quarters and placed them on the counter next to Kyle. He was ladling the fragrant vegetable soup into bowls, but she'd lost her appetite.

Kyle tugged a tall stool up to the counter and mo-

tioned for her to sit. He pulled another stool next to
hers and settled down to eat. He swallowed a bite of
sandwich. "Did you know Gary Bowen has a gambling problem?"

"Was that in Daddy's files?"

Kyle shook his head. "I faxed the names and social security numbers of everyone on the staff to
Court last night. He's running background checks
and has already uncovered that Gary Bowen is deep
in debt. The gambling connection was easy to uncover."

"But Gary and his wife are just kids. I can't imagine either of them involved with the Black Order."
Laura broke a crust of her sandwich and crumbled it
with her fingers as a thought struck her. "You suspect everyone, don't you?"

Kyle had finished his soup, his appetite obviously
unaffected by the gravity of their conversation. "Until we find the real informant."

"Does that include me?"

Her heart plummeted at his sudden stillness. With
his forest-green gaze boring into hers, he reached
across the counter and took her hand. The heat of his
body accentuated the coldness of her skin.

"I won't lie to you, Laura. We considered that
possibility in the beginning."

The idea that anyone could think her capable of
helping her father's murderers sickened her. "And
what conclusions did you reach?"

"We believe you're an unlikely suspect."

"Unlikely? But you haven't ruled me out?" Out-
rage boiled inside her.

Kyle's gaze didn't waver. "We can't rule anyone out completely until we have our informant under arrest—"

She tried to yank her hand away, but he held it firm. She twisted her head to avoid his eyes, but he slid from the stool, grasped her chin gently in his fingers and turned her face toward him.

"I wouldn't be here, married to you," he said, "if I had any doubts. I've put my life in your hands."

The truth of his words and the earnestness of his expression dissolved her anger. Hovering just inches away, he dropped his gaze to her lips, and she thought for an instant that he was going to kiss her again. When he pulled away instead, disappointment washed over her.

"Eat your lunch. You'll need your strength." He gave her shoulder a friendly pat. "You must try not to let my investigation upset you."

Because he seemed genuinely concerned about her, she sipped her soup. "Find any other skeletons in our staff closet?" she asked.

"Dr. Kwan and Wayne Pritchard seem squeaky clean, but Dr. Potter belonged to some questionable organizations during his college days."

Dismayed, she dropped her spoon into the bowl. "Uncle Bob?"

"You're related?"

"Not really. But I've known him all my life. My father and he went to college together." An unpleasant thought struck her, and she felt her eyes widen. "In fact, Daddy belonged to those same 'questionable organizations' you mentioned."

A pained expression flitted across Kyle's handsome features. "We know."

"Good grief, you don't suspect *Daddy?*"

As if suddenly uncomfortable, he shifted on his seat. "We haven't ruled out any suspects yet."

Her earlier anger paled compared to the fiery rage that consumed her now. "If you think I'm going to help you frame my father—"

"Whoa, hold on." His green eyes reminded her of storm-tossed seas, and he appeared to be fighting to maintain his self-control. "I'm not pointing the finger at anyone, but to do my job right, I have to cover all the bases. That includes checking your father's background and all his contacts. If Josiah is innocent—"

"If?"

"—you have nothing to worry about." He shook his head, clearly frustrated. "Look, Laura, someone has used his or her connections to your father to access the biological weapons at the lab. We have to investigate everyone to find out who that person is. I believe your father, if he were here, would support what we're doing."

She pushed away her plate and laid her head on her arms, folded on the counter. "I guess I'm not as tough as I thought I was."

Suddenly she found herself gathered up in Kyle's arms, her face pressed against the broad expanse of his chest, his head against her hair. She could feel the thud of his heartbeat against her cheek, and she welcomed the security of his embrace. Feeling like a tiny boat floundering on heavy seas, she considered the warmth of Kyle's arms a port in the storm.

Nothing in her life was going the way she had planned. She had thought Curt's infidelity the cruelest blow—until her father was killed. She hadn't planned on running the Institute alone. And she certainly hadn't counted on falling in love again.

Falling in love?

She jerked away from Kyle's embrace as if she'd been burned. Hadn't she learned anything from her disastrous marriage? If she gave her heart to Kyle, he could walk away when his informant was caught. Or worse yet, what if he insisted on tying her father to the Black Order?

She felt ripped apart. Half of her wanted to fling herself back into Kyle's strong arms. The other half wanted him to go away. The distinctive chime of the front doorbell saved her from making a choice.

KYLE BENT OVER the gleaming dining-room table to study the aerial photographs and layouts of the Institute that Monty Slater had spread there. Slater's arrival had interrupted Kyle's discussion with Laura, but it was just as well. When Laura had pulled away, Kyle had been tempted to draw her back, to reassure with kisses the doubts that clouded her magnificent eyes. Better, however, that Laura remained angry with him. Her indignation would keep him at a distance, the best place for him if he wanted to keep a clear head and his wits about him.

Resolved to focus on his assignment, Kyle turned his attention back to Slater. The retired FBI agent, now head of his own security service, still dressed the part of a government agent. Instead of the customary Montana uniform of jeans, he wore a dark business suit, dazzling white dress shirt and muted silk tie. The clothes couldn't hide, however, his muscular build and obvious fitness, extraordinary for a man in his sixties, or the slight bulge of a firearm holstered beneath his jacket.

Slater raked his slender fingers through his graying blond hair and pointed to the aerial photograph. "Daniel gave me this and the other layouts when I met with him at the ranch this morning. We put together a proposal to augment your current security, but Daniel insisted you have the final say."

Kyle nodded. "What do you suggest?"

"First, two-man teams at the gate."

"Agreed," Kyle said. "The gate's a weak point."

Slater drew a well-manicured hand around the perimeter. "And two-man teams with K-9s to patrol the fence."

On the other side of the table, Laura spoke. "The sheriff says the terrorists cut the fence to steal the D-5."

Slater cast a questioning glance at Kyle.

"You can speak freely," Kyle said. "Laura's one of the good guys."

Kyle met her blue-eyed gaze head-on, silently reminding her that he had no suspicions where she was concerned. She blushed prettily under the force of his stare and turned her attention to Slater.

The security man nodded. "The sheriff could be wrong about the fence."

Alarm deepened the red in Laura's cheeks. "What do you mean?"

Slater shrugged. "It's equally possible the fence was cut to make it *look* like an outside job. Someone on the inside could have forced the locks on the storage refrigerator and carried out the D-5 in their car. Your gate guard says he hasn't been instructed to inspect personal vehicles."

"It may seem like locking the barn door once the horse has escaped," Laura said, "but I think those storage areas in the lab should be protected."

"I agree," Slater said. "Teams of three in three shifts twenty-four/seven at the lab."

"That's going to run into a big chunk of change," Kyle noted.

Slater shrugged. "Good protection doesn't come cheap. Every one of my employees is thoroughly checked and vetted."

"Cost doesn't matter," Laura insisted. "I just want everyone and the biological weapon samples kept safe until these terrorists are behind bars."

"Then may I make another suggestion?" Looking more like a banker than an ex-agent, Slater smoothed his tie and buttoned his jacket. He turned to Kyle. "Daniel says you're bringing your daughter to live here."

"Only if I can guarantee her safety."

"Understood," Slater said. "That's why I want to place Bonnie Shapiro in this house."

"Won't a bodyguard send a signal to the informant that we suspect an inside job?" Kyle said.

Slater shook his head. "Bonnie won't be associated with security. As far as the rest of the people here are concerned, you've hired her as a combination nanny-housekeeper.''

"What can Bonnie do in looking after Molly that I can't?'' Laura asked.

A slow smile spread like sunshine across Slater's aging face. "No disrespect intended, Mrs. Foster, but Bonnie is six feet, a hundred and eighty pounds of pure muscle. She's trained in all the martial arts, she's an excellent shot and there's nothing on this planet she's afraid of.''

Laura frowned. "She won't scare Molly?''

Kyle had wondered the same thing, but Laura had beat him to the punch in asking. Her obvious affection for Molly was only one of the qualities he admired in Laura, and at her aggressive concern for his daughter, he found his objectivity slipping once again.

"Bonnie is wonderful with children,'' Slater said. "She's just returned from South America where she guarded the children of a U.S. diplomat in Chile.''

Kyle still had second thoughts about bringing Molly to the Institute. He loved his job and was committed to it, but he wouldn't place his child in danger. "Even if Bonnie is the best, she has to sleep sometime. Who's going to guard Molly then?''

"I have another agent who can pose as your chauffeur. I notice there's an apartment over the garage. He can live there during the day, but spend nights inside the house. That way you'll all sleep easier.''

Kyle glanced at Laura. "What do you think?''

She gave Slater one of her megawatt smiles. "You

seem to have thought of everything. If Kyle agrees, your plan sounds good to me.''

''How soon can you have everyone in place?'' Kyle asked.

Slater began rolling up the photographs and diagrams. ''Tomorrow morning—''

In the foyer behind them, the front door opened and slammed against the inner wall with a bang. Kyle moved swiftly between the dining-room door and Laura. From the corner of his eye, he saw Slater reach beneath his jacket for his gun.

Before Slater could draw, a short plump woman with dark hair laced with gray stumbled into the room. Laura stepped around Kyle and went to her.

''Zahra, what's happened?''

The woman's dark eyes were wide with fear, and she waved her hands in agitation. ''Lawrence.''

''What's happened?'' Kyle asked. ''Is Dr. Tyson ill?''

Zahra shook her head, and tears pooled in her eyes. ''He's gone.''

Laura placed her arms around the older woman. ''Gone?''

''Disappeared,'' Zahra sobbed. ''No one knows what's happened to him.''

Chapter Nine

Kyle took the hysterical Zahra Tyson by the arm, led her into the living room and settled her in a comfortable chair. Laura and Slater followed.

"Want me to call the sheriff?" Slater asked.

Zahra shook her head. "Gary—my husband's research assistant has already called him."

"Call Daniel," Kyle asked the security man with a pointed look.

Slater pulled a cell phone from his jacket and stepped out onto the front porch to make his call.

Laura perched on the arm of the chair and hugged the grieving woman's shoulders. Kyle admired her warm compassion and calm demeanor in the face of Zahra's distress. Laura was more than just a pretty face. She had a heart of gold. He cursed inwardly. She was too good a woman to suffer all that fate had thrown at her.

"Now, Zahra," Laura said soothingly, "tell us exactly what happened."

The woman pulled a tissue from the pocket of her sweater, wiped her red-rimmed eyes and blew her nose. "Lawrence didn't come home to lunch." She forced a watery smile. "Sometimes he gets so immersed in his work, he forgets what time it is. So I telephoned the lab and asked Gary to remind him. Gary called back a few minutes later and said he couldn't locate Lawrence, that he must be on his way home."

Zahra's hands shook, and she clasped them tightly in her lap. "After a while, when Lawrence still hadn't arrived, I called the lab again. Gary said he'd look for him."

"Maybe he drove into town," Kyle suggested.

"We only have one car. It's in the condo garage."

"He could have caught a ride with someone else."

The older woman shook her head and swallowed a sob. "Gary called the gatehouse. The guard said no one's left the compound all day."

Laura patted Zahra's hand. "At his age, he could have had a small stroke that disoriented him, and he's wandered off. We'll find him."

The sudden ringing of a telephone startled them all.

"I'll get it," Kyle said with an encouraging smile. "It's probably your husband, wondering where you are."

He hurried into the kitchen where he could talk on the extension without being overheard.

"Dr. Foster?" an unfamiliar male voice asked.

"Yes."

"This is Gary Bowen."

Kyle pictured the red-haired, hyperactive young man he'd met at the morning staff conference, the assistant with the gambling problem. "Have you found Dr. Tyson?"

"No, sir. But we've discovered Dr. Tyson isn't the only thing missing."

The urgency in the research assistant's tone was impossible for Kyle to overlook. "Someone else is gone?"

"Wayne, the other lab assistant, went to the refrigerated storage locker a few minutes ago to collect some vials for Dr. Kwan. Another sample's disappeared."

Icy apprehension spread through Kyle's gut. "More D-5?"

"Worse, sir. An especially nasty mutated form of anthrax. There's no antidote for it."

Kyle leaned his head against the cold stainless steel of the refrigerator door. If the Black Order was behind the theft, they now had two lethal biological weapons in their arsenal.

He turned his attention back to Gary. "Mrs. Tyson said you've called the sheriff."

"Yes, sir. He and a team of deputies are on the way."

"I'll meet you at the lab shortly. Have the staff do a quick inventory of the other storage areas. Make sure nothing else is missing."

"Yes, sir."

Kyle hung up the receiver and turned at the sound of footsteps. Monty Slater walked into the kitchen, his face grim. "I've talked to Daniel. He and Frank are on their way. Frank will say C.J. called and asked him to help search for Dr. Tyson. He'll bring Daniel along as a friend who volunteered. That way, the Confidential agents' cover won't be compromised.''

Kyle filled Slater in on Gary's phone call.

The security man grimaced. ''I'll step up our plans and have those extra guards in place this evening.''

Kyle flashed him a rueful smile. ''A little late for that, isn't it?''

''At least you'll have more security while you and the sheriff conduct your investigation. You don't want to lose any more biological weapons.''

AN HOUR AND A HALF LATER, Kyle tramped the inside perimeter of the compound fence with Daniel and Court, looking for signs of Dr. Tyson, while the sheriff's deputies searched the lab and condos. Laura had stayed at the house with Mrs. Tyson. The uneven terrain made Frank's limp a little more pronounced, but it didn't slow the big man down. Daniel hiked beside him, a Winchester rifle ready in the crook of his arm, ostensibly for rattlesnakes.

''Odd that Tyson should disappear the same day you showed up here,'' Daniel said.

''He was agitated at the meeting this morning,'' Kyle said. ''Accused me of being a fraud.''

With a look of alarm, Daniel straightened from his scrutiny of the path. ''He didn't believe your cover?''

''He didn't believe I am experienced enough to function here. Whether he suspected I'm not really a scientist working in biological warfare, I couldn't tell.''

''Hey, guys!'' Frank shouted from a few feet ahead. ''Take a look at this.''

Kyle and Daniel hurried up the path that paralleled the inside of the fence to where Frank stood beside a scrubby bush. When they reached him, he pushed aside the branches to reveal a man-size hole in the chain-link fence.

Daniel leaned over and inspected the breach. "Bolt cutters."

"This isn't where the Black Order entered the first time?" Kyle asked.

Frank shook his head. "That was closer to the condos, and that gap has been repaired."

Daniel ran his finger over a severed wire. "There's no oxidation on the metal. These cuts are recent."

Kyle nudged an object in the grass with the toe of his boot. "Here're your bolt cutters. I'll have the sheriff's boys bag them for prints."

Frank frowned. "You think an intruder dumped the tool once he was inside?"

"From the angle of these cuts," Daniel said, "looks like someone was going out, not coming in."

"That leaves us with two possibilities," Frank said. "Either Tyson's been kidnapped, possibly by someone who came in *over* the fence—"

"Gary Bowen said there was no sign of a struggle at the lab," Kyle reminded him.

"The other scenario," Frank added, "is that Tyson's our informant and he's making a getaway."

Kyle moved away to keep from contaminating the area for the crime technicians and settled on a large boulder. "I don't get it. I don't see how my arrival here could have spooked anyone. My cover is sound."

Daniel squatted on his muscular haunches beside Kyle and chewed thoughtfully on a blade of dried grass. "Maybe Monty and his security truck rattled the informant."

"Slater didn't get here until after lunch," Kyle said. "According to Tyson's wife, he was missing a good hour before that."

Daniel's brown eyes narrowed. "Maybe somebody tipped off the informant that Slater was coming, that security would be tightened."

"Impossible," Kyle said. "We're the only ones who knew, unless you think Slater leaked it."

"I'd trust Monty with my life." Daniel's expression was fierce with loyalty. "In fact, I have, several times in the past."

Frank looked uncomfortable. "There's one other person who knew about the plans to increase security."

"Who?" Kyle asked.

Frank didn't meet his gaze. "Laura."

"Aw, get real." Kyle shook his head. He didn't even have to think about Frank's accusation. He felt the answer deep in his gut. And his heart. "Laura's no traitor."

"Then we're back where we started." Daniel stood and tossed the blade of grass aside. "There's only one way to get the answers we need. We have to find Tyson."

A COMPLETE EXAMINATION of the perimeter and the surrounding woods revealed no sign of the elderly scientist. Nor did the deputies turn up anything in their inspection of the lab and condos. A swiftly moving cold front complete with icy rain and gathering darkness brought an end to the search. The deputies suspended their investigation for the night, Daniel and Frank drove back to the Lonesome Pony and Kyle returned to Laura's house.

He entered through the rear door and shed his wet jacket in the mudroom, careful to conceal the papers in its pocket. He hoped he'd never have to tell Laura about them. The sheriff had given him copies of a file they'd found in the back of a drawer in Lawrence Tyson's desk. The papers implicated both Tyson and Josiah as collaborators with the Black Order. Kyle knew that if Laura found out about her father's complicity, it would break her heart.

Laura met him in the kitchen. "Any luck?"

He shook his head. "We found a breach in the fence, but no sign of Tyson."

With a tender smile that made him regret the discovery of Josiah's treachery even more, she lifted her hand to his cheek. "You're a block of ice. I've built a fire in the family room. You can thaw out there, and I'll bring you something hot to drink."

Thankful for the glowing heat, he collapsed his tired bones onto the deep sofa that fronted the fireplace and propped his damp boots on the coffee table. He could hear Laura moving around in the kitchen behind him, and a moment later she handed him a steaming mug.

"Hot buttered rum," she said.

He gave her a grateful smile. "Woman, I think you just saved my miserable life."

She grinned. "Now we're even."

She curled into the corner of the sofa next to him, kicking off her shoes and folding her long legs gracefully beneath her. Her beautiful features settled into somber lines, and her eyes darkened to midnight blue. "What's going on, Kyle?"

He sipped his toddy, and its hot warmth flooded through him. She'd laced it with enough rum to supply a battleship. "Looks like Tyson was either kidnapped or stole the anthrax and took off on his own."

He couldn't tell her that, from the papers in the file that were found in Tyson's office, the latter appeared most likely. She'd find out soon enough. And then she'd have to learn about her father's guilt, too. When that time came, he hoped someone else, maybe Daniel, could reveal the awful truth. Kyle couldn't stand the thought of hurting her, and it would be even worse if he was the one who had to do it.

She wrinkled her forehead. "It doesn't make sense."

"What?"

"That the Black Order's had the D-5 for over a month, and they haven't used it. They haven't even threatened to use it—not that I'm not glad. It just seems strange."

Kyle nodded. "Daniel and Frank and I discussed that, and we have a theory."

She leaned toward him, and the scent of orange blossoms blended with the aroma of buttered rum. He wanted to draw her close and hold her, to protect her from the pain she was sure to suffer when she learned the truth about her father. He draped his arm around her shoulders, and she scooted easily to his side with her head against his shoulder. Her presence was even more effective than the scalding toddy in driving away the cold that gripped him.

"What's your theory?" she asked.

"It isn't pretty."

"Nothing about this business is."

You are, he thought, but didn't say it. She would hate him by the time the investigation ended. Along with the sheriff's department and the Confidential agents, Kyle would be among those who had proved her father a traitor to his country.

"And our theory has its flaws."

"At least it's a start," she said. "Tell me."

"Weston, the senator from Montana, is running for president on an antiterrorism platform, and the election is only weeks away."

She nodded. "The senator's been our biggest ally in Congress. We owe almost all the federal support for the Institute to his influence."

"What if the terrorists want to make certain he's not elected?"

Her magnificent blue eyes widened. "Dear God. You think they're waiting to use the D-5 to influence the election?"

"Maybe. If they can wreak havoc and kill thousands in Weston's home state, they would show the nation the Black Order's not afraid of him, make him seem ineffective. That might be why they chose to bomb the Montana capitol instead of a more strategic target. To embarrass Weston."

She sat quietly for a while, as if thinking. "But couldn't that strategy backfire? Make people so angry at the terrorists that they'd vote Weston in, since he's the one who has vowed to get them?"

His admiration increased. Laura Quinlan was one smart woman. She'd grasped the paradox immediately.

"I told you the theory was flawed."

She raised her hand and caressed his cheek. "You're no longer a block of ice. How about some supper?"

His face was inches from hers, and he could feel the warmth of her breath against his skin. The pupils of her eyes widened beneath his gaze, and his own breathing quickened. He wanted to cherish this woman, protect her from the horrors that swirled around them.

The rum must have lowered his inhibitions and short-circuited his commonsense, and he couldn't help himself. He dipped his head and tasted her lips. Shifting her onto his lap, he wrapped his arms around her and pulled her against him. In the heat of their embrace, he forgot about his damp clothes, his tired muscles, the incriminating papers in the pocket of his jacket. All that existed in the world was the woman in his arms. Their kiss was long and deep and tender, and when she finally pulled away, her look was questioning with a hint of wonder glinting in her eyes.

Her luscious mouth quirked into a knee-weakening smile, and her eyes twinkled with mischief. "Was there someone watching?"

Sizzling warmth and an unexpected happiness

flooded through him. "You never know. There could be somebody hiding under the couch."

She snuggled against him. "This is nice."

And crazy, he reminded himself.

He shouldn't care so much for her, couldn't allow her to care for him. Once she learned of Josiah's treachery, their relationship was doomed.

But as hard as he tried, he couldn't force himself to his feet, couldn't thrust her from his arms. With a contentment that he knew was temporary and definitely not smart, he held her in his arms while the fire burned low.

THE FOLLOWING MORNING, Kyle and Laura climbed into the Institute SUV to drive to the ranch to pick up Molly. Bonnie Shapiro had arrived an hour before, and Laura had helped the nanny-bodyguard settle in the guest bedroom. Rick Cope, combination chauffeur and night watchman, had moved into the apartment over the garage. Even so, Kyle had his doubts about removing Molly from the safety of the ranch.

"Do you really think she'll be in danger here?" Laura asked.

He glanced into the rearview mirror at the director's house receding into the distance. "Slater swears both Bonnie and Rick will protect her with their lives. I'd just feel a lot better if I knew what happened to Dr. Tyson."

They approached the gatehouse and stopped before the lowered crossbar.

One of Slater's two-man team stepped to the

driver's window. "Identification, please, and pop the rear hatch."

Kyle and Laura produced their Institute ID cards, and Kyle watched with satisfaction while the second guard made a thorough search of the vehicle's interior.

Their duties fulfilled, the guards raised the crossbar and waved the SUV through.

"That should make you feel better," Laura said. "At least no one who isn't supposed to will get in or out by the gate."

Kyle shook his head. "I still have qualms about bringing Molly into this."

Laura reached across the well between the seats and placed her hand on his arm. He could feel her warmth through his sleeve, and memories of last night, holding her in his arms before the fire, threatened to distract him.

"If you aren't sure," she said gravely, "perhaps you should leave her with Dale and Jewel at the ranch until the Black Order members are caught."

Kyle grimaced. "Catching terrorists isn't always a speedy process. It could take months. Besides, I don't want her to be away from me. Not after last night."

"What happened?" Laura's throaty voice rose an octave.

"She cried when I told her good-night on the phone last night." Recalling her sobs, her tearful pleas, his heart ached like a broken bone. "She misses me. And I miss her."

"Then you're definitely doing the right thing," Laura said, "or else you'll both be miserable."

Laura sounded so certain, but Kyle still wasn't sure. He was already distracted enough by Laura Quinlan. They had fallen asleep in each other's arms in front of the fire the previous night, just like a real married couple. When they'd awakened, he'd wanted nothing more than to carry her upstairs to the king-size bed in the master suite. He'd needed every ounce of self-restraint to stand and stretch and pretend nothing had happened, that he hadn't relished sleeping with Laura in his arms, and that he didn't wish he'd done more than just sleep.

Laura had fixed them supper, and she, too, had acted as if nothing out of the ordinary had occurred, but Kyle knew better. The air between them had zinged with electricity, and he'd had to fight the urge to kiss her good-night. He'd struggled all over again a few hours ago to keep from kissing her good-morning. With Laura attracting him like a flame lures a moth, and with Molly's safety to worry about, he'd do well to remember his own name, much less uncover what happened to Tyson or track down the traitor at the Institute.

His situation went from bad to worse when they arrived at the ranch. As they stepped out of the SUV, Molly raced to greet him on chubby legs.

"Daddy! Daddy! You've been gone *forever*." Her tiny arms rounded his neck in a stranglehold that almost cut off his air, and she covered his face with kisses.

"Hey, doodlebug. How's my favorite daughter?"

She leaned back in his arms, took his face in her hands and grinned. "Better now, Daddy. I missed you."

"I missed you, too, sweetheart." With Molly in his arms, Kyle turned toward Laura. "You remember Miss Laura."

Molly nodded solemnly. "Hello."

"Hello, yourself." Laura opened her arms. "May I have a kiss, too?"

Molly nodded. Kyle handed her to Laura, and Molly planted a noisy kiss on Laura's cheek that made Laura's pretty face light up like a mountain sunrise. She set the little girl on her feet and took one of her hands, and Kyle took the other. Together the three walked toward the main house. Yesterday's rain had left the air clean, clear and warmed by sunshine in spite of the chilly temperature.

"Let's sit on the steps, doodlebug," Kyle said. "Daddy has something to tell you."

Molly sank onto the steps between Kyle and Laura and gazed up at her father with worried green eyes, her tiny mouth pinched in a frown. "Are you going away again?"

He hugged her to him. "I'm going back to live at Laura's, but you'll be coming, too."

"Leave the ranch?" Molly asked.

"Laura and I were married—"

"You had a wedding?"

Kyle nodded.

Molly's eyes teared. "Wif'out me?"

The little girl burst into racking sobs. Panicked by Molly's distress, he glanced to Laura for help, but she appeared as unequipped as he felt to deal with his daughter's unexpected outburst.

Between them, Molly wailed, "I wanted to be a f'ower girl. Jewel said if you got married, I could be a f'ower girl."

Laura pulled the sobbing Molly onto her lap and stroked her curly hair. "It wasn't that kind of wedding, Molly. It wasn't in a church with flowers and bridesmaids. We were married in a judge's office."

"But I *wanted* to be a f'ower girl."

Kyle was out of his element. He'd never seen Molly so distressed, and weddings and flower girls were as foreign to him as outer space. "What can we do?"

"We'll have a big party," Laura said, aiming her words at Molly. "You can wear a special dress, a very pretty dress with bows and ruffles, just like a flower girl's, and you'll carry a big basketful of flowers and hand them out to all the guests. Would you like that?"

Molly's sobs slowly subsided into sniffles. "What color dress?"

Laura smiled. "What color would you like?"

Molly scrunched her face in thought. "Yellow."

"We'll find you the prettiest yellow dress in Montana," Kyle promised, and shot Laura a grateful look. "But first, we have to move you to our new house."

"Is Ribbons coming, too?" Molly's chubby cheeks were streaked with tears.

Kyle, fearing more waterworks were imminent,

braced himself. "Laura doesn't have a stable at her house."

Molly's lips quivered.

"Not yet." Laura jumped in quickly with reassurance. "But we'll build a place for Ribbons, and until it's ready, I'll bring you back to the ranch several times a week to visit Ribbons and take your rides."

Molly wiped tears from her cheeks with the backs of her hands and gazed up at Laura. "Are you my new mommy?"

Laura looked at Kyle with the spooked expression of a nocturnal animal caught in a sudden beam of light.

"That's right, doodlebug," he said. "Laura's your new mommy."

A broad grin stretched across Molly's face. "Good."

Now Laura looked as if she was going to cry.

With an overwhelming sense of relief, Kyle stood and lifted Molly in his arms. "Let's load your clothes and toys in the car."

A half hour later, Kyle had stowed the last of Molly's belongings in the car. Bubbly and excited once her initial tears had passed, Molly had said her goodbyes to Daniel, Dale and Jewel. Laura fastened Molly into her child carrier in the back seat, then slid into the passenger seat beside Kyle. He put the SUV in gear and headed down the driveway toward the highway.

"Is our new house big?" Molly asked.

"A lot bigger than our cabin at the ranch." Kyle

relaxed now that Molly's good spirits had returned and she seemed to be looking forward to the move.

"Bigger than Daniel's house?" Molly said.

"Not quite that big," Laura answered, "but more than big enough for the three of us."

For the remainder of the drive, Laura described the house to Molly, paying particular detail to Molly's room. She also explained that Bonnie Shapiro would be helping at her new home, much like Dale McMurty assisted Daniel at the ranch. By the time they passed through the gate, Molly was bouncing in her car seat with excitement, and Kyle's reservations about taking Molly off the ranch had dwindled.

His fears returned in force, however, when he pulled into the driveway of the director's house and glanced down the road. Deputies were loading a team of dogs into a sheriff's K-9 van. As Kyle climbed out of the SUV, a deputy approached him.

"Dr. Foster?"

"Yes."

"Can I speak with you in private?"

Kyle nodded to Laura who hurried Molly inside the house. With relief, Kyle noted that Molly was skipping and babbling happily the entire way. Once the door had closed behind them, Kyle turned to the deputy. "What's this all about?"

The deputy's expression was somber. "We've found Dr. Tyson."

Chapter Ten

Kyle turned the shower to its heaviest pulse, let the hot water batter his aches and tiredness and wished he could cleanse away bitterness and despair as easily. He'd spent the afternoon hunched in a culvert beneath the road that ran behind the lab. His muscles screamed in protest from the prolonged cramped posture, his head reeled with unanswered questions and his conscience goaded him for deserting Molly on her first day in new surroundings.

Upping the water temperature to scalding, he rinsed the stench of muck and death from his body and wished he could sluice away his problems as well. With a violent flick of his wrist, he shut off the water then stepped from the huge glassed-in shower in the master bath and grabbed a towel.

He wrapped the fluffy terry cloth around his waist, then used another towel to rub the dripping moisture from his hair. He jerked back in surprise when two green eyes so like his own met him almost on his own level.

"Hi, Daddy." Molly, standing on the closed toilet lid, peered through the steam with an impish grin.

"Hey, doodlebug." She was wearing her favorite flannel nightgown and hugging the stuffed dog she'd named Scooter. "Ready for bed?"

She nodded. "Bonnie fixed my supper."

A voice rang out in the adjoining bedroom. "Molly, where are—"

Laura skidded to a stop just inside the bathroom door. Her glance slid quickly over Kyle's towel-clad torso, then fastened on his daughter. A delightful flush inched its way up her neck and reddened her cheeks, but whether from embarrassment or the sauna-like conditions of the room, he couldn't tell.

"Sorry," Laura said. "I didn't know you'd come in."

"Sneaked in the back," he said. "Needed to clean up before I was fit for human company."

"Come, Molly, I'll tuck you in while your daddy gets dressed." Without a backward look, Laura scooped Molly into her arms and headed toward the door.

"Read me a story," Molly was insisting as they passed through the master bedroom. "Padd'ton Bear."

Kyle watched them go with a catch in his heart. The way Laura interacted with his daughter created a warm glow of contentment deep inside him. He wanted Molly with him, but he wanted to spare both Molly and Laura the horror he'd witnessed that afternoon. He would keep the facts from Molly. She was too little to understand.

Laura would have to know.

With a sigh of resignation, he tugged on clean

jeans, a fresh shirt and a pair of deck shoes that would have to suffice until he could scour the culvert mud off his boots. Slicking back his wet hair, he tucked in his shirt and headed down the hall toward Molly's room.

He drew up short in the doorway, a knot of emotion in his throat. The tranquil scene before him reminded him exactly of why he'd become a cop, why he fought now against the scourge of hatred and terrorism. Laura sat among pillows propped against the headboard with Molly in her lap. His daughter turned the pages of the book as Laura read.

"What are val'ble chunks?" Molly asked.

Laura bent over the book with her dark hair hiding her face, but he could hear the smile in her melodic voice as she pointed to a picture on the page. "That's what Paddington calls marmalade."

"What's marm'ade?"

Kyle grinned with contentment. It was good to have Molly back, even if she had reached the stage when almost everything she said formed a question.

"Marmalade is like jelly," Laura explained. "It's made from oranges. You can have some on your toast for breakfast tomorrow."

"Want me to tuck you in?" Kyle asked.

At the sound of his voice, Molly looked up and smiled. "Uh-huh. And Laura, too."

Laura had apparently regained her composure after he'd surprised her in the bathroom. "You look good with your clothes on."

Teasing caused a delightful glint in her eyes and tugged at the dimple on her cheek, a spot that looked eminently kissable. He reined in his impulses and assumed a pout. "Are you implying they're an improvement?"

"Clothes make the man, or so they say."

"They," he said with an exaggerated leer and a suggestive jiggle of his eyebrows, "have never seen *me* in a towel."

Molly giggled. "You're silly, Daddy."

"And you're up past your bedtime, doodlebug." He crossed the room, lifted the sheet and blankets on the twin bed and waited while Molly scrambled between them. Then he tucked the blankets around her, brushed her blond curls off her forehead and planted a kiss there. "Sleep tight, sweetheart."

On the other side of the bed, Laura leaned over and kissed Molly's cheek.

"Night-night, Daddy, Miss Laura," Molly said sleepily, her eyelids drooping.

Kyle turned out the bedside lamp and followed Laura to the door.

"I left a night-light burning." Laura headed down the back stairs toward the kitchen, and Kyle trailed along behind. "I don't want her to be afraid when she wakes up in a strange place."

"You've been great with her. Especially since I had to take off as soon as we got here. I'm sorry about that."

"Bonnie took care of her." They entered the kitchen, and Laura stopped at the refrigerator door. "They hit it off right away. Here's the picture of Ribbons Molly drew for Bonnie."

Kyle studied the crayon scribble, an indecipherable bubble with stick legs, big eyes and a flowing tail. Picasso couldn't have done better.

"You weren't here this afternoon?" he asked.

"Not the whole time. When C.J. called from the lab and said they'd found Lawrence's body, I went over to Zahra's to stay with her until C.J. finished work and came to relieve me. Melinda Kwan will spend the night there. Zahra's sister arrives tomorrow."

Kyle ran his fingers over the scar in his eyebrow. It always itched worst when he was tired. "How much do you know?"

Her expression was somber. "Almost nothing, except that Lawrence is dead. I'll pour us some wine, and you can fill me in while supper finishes cooking."

"Where's Bonnie?"

"She ate with Molly, then went to her room to watch television."

More exhausted than he'd realized, Kyle accepted a glass of Chardonnay and sank into the cushions of the sofa in front of the fireplace. Laura added another log to the fire, then settled beside him.

"Lawrence was murdered," he said.

"You're sure it wasn't an accident? He didn't wander from the lab and fall or something?" Her eyes swam with pain, begging him to agree with her.

"According to the coroner, someone broke his neck, then dumped his body in the culvert."

At his graphic description, she flinched so hard she sloshed wine from her glass.

"I'm sorry," he said. "There's no easy way to tell

this. If not for the cadaver dogs, we wouldn't have found Dr. Tyson's body for days, maybe weeks.''

''And the anthrax?''

''Not a trace.''

She dabbed at the spilled wine with a napkin, then twirled the stem of her glass between slender fingers. Even when upset, she was beautiful, her eyes dark with despair, her translucent skin pale with grief, her usually smooth forehead creased with worry. He reached for her hand and squeezed it gently in an effort to console her.

''At least we know Lawrence wasn't our traitor,'' she said with a deep sigh. ''That's some comfort.''

Kyle thought of the incriminating papers found in Tyson's desk, but held his tongue. Laura was upset enough over the scientist's death. She shouldn't have to deal with the probability that he *had* been the Black Order informant, or the suspicion that the terrorists had killed him once he'd outlived his usefulness.

''We'll know more once the investigation's finished,'' he said.

''How much longer?''

Kyle sighed. Despite knowing that terrorists were elusive and difficult to track, he was impatient to end their reign of terror. ''We have yet to find a connection that leads us to the Black Order. With the D-5 and anthrax in their possession, it's more important than ever that we track them down.'' Turning her hand palm upward, he traced its delicate lines with his finger and attempted to lighten the conversation. ''Anxious to get rid of me?''

She withdrew her hand, tucked her legs beneath her on the sofa and shifted to face him with an enigmatic smile. "I like having you and Molly here. Makes it seem more like a home. But I admit to an ulterior motive to my question."

She reached behind her on the sofa table and picked up an envelope of heavy linen paper, addressed in impressive calligraphy to Dr. and Mrs. Kyle Foster. A gold seal on the flap had been broken. She handed it to him.

"What's this?" he asked.

"Read it."

He lifted the flap then tugged out an engraved invitation and scanned it. "An invitation to a party? In Washington, D.C.?"

"Senator Weston's been one of the Institute's biggest supporters. He keeps close tabs on everything that happens here. He's pushed the majority of our funding through Congress, and this is his last big fling before the election next month. We'll have to go."

Kyle returned the invitation to her. "You can go. I have an investigation to complete."

A shadow of disappointment darkened her lovely features. "You're right, of course. Your investigation should come first. But won't it look strange for us as newlyweds if you stay here while I go to Washington?"

"To be honest, even if I didn't have an investigation, I wouldn't go."

"Don't tell me you're antisocial."

"Antisocial? No, but I'd rather be smeared with

honey and staked to an anthill than attend a Washington party.''

Right now, Kyle didn't want to go anywhere. He laid his head against the back of the sofa and closed his eyes. He was so tired his bones ached, and even more grueling than his physical activities had been his state of constant alertness maintaining his cover as a working scientist and Laura's new husband.

All he wanted now was sleep.

He drifted into unconsciousness, and he couldn't tell if Laura's brief kiss that fluttered across his lips when she rose from the sofa was real or just a very pleasant dream.

SEVERAL DAYS LATER, Laura turned her attention from the billowing clouds outside the plane window to Kyle, sitting beside her. Ever since they'd boarded the plane for Washington, he'd been studying the files and notes he'd brought with him. Although he'd been adamant about remaining at the Institute for the weekend instead of attending the Senator's party, a phone call from Daniel had changed his mind.

The head of Montana Confidential had forcefully reminded Kyle that not only was Senator Weston the Quinlan Institute's greatest supporter in Congress, he was also leading the vanguard for federal funding to fight terrorism. In effect, Weston was the man most responsible for the salaries and expense accounts that kept Montana Confidential functioning. For Kyle to ignore the senator's invitation would be not only politically incorrect, it could be economic suicide for the agency.

She smiled, remembering their subsequent hasty jaunt into Livingston to buy a tuxedo. Molly had gone with them and had giggled when Kyle stepped out of the dressing room.

Laughing had been the farthest thing from Laura's mind. The well-fitted evening wear had transformed Kyle's rugged good looks into a sexy smoothness and elegance that would have made an Academy Award–winning actor proud. The resulting flutter of her heart distressed her. She was becoming entirely too fond of Kyle and his daughter, and unless she brought her emotions under control, she was certain to suffer the devastation of loneliness once the terrorists were caught and the Fosters moved out of her life.

"Daddy, you look like a pinkwin."

"And I feel like an idiot. Why do men wear these things?"

He caught sight of Laura's grin and held up his hands. "You don't have to answer that. I know why. Women insist on it."

Laura had tried to remain serious, but her lips kept curving in a smile. "Now, Kyle, you know even a died-in-the-wool Montanan like Weston will take offense if you show up at his formal party in boots and blue jeans."

Kyle ran a finger under the collar of the white shirt and grimaced. "I could go buck naked and an important man like Weston wouldn't even notice me."

Laura's smile expanded. "Now there's an enticing idea."

Molly's eyes widened. "You're going to the party with no clothes?"

"No, doodlebug. I'll wear this, even if I do look like a penguin."

Molly clapped her chubby hands. "But you're a nice pinkwin, Daddy."

Laura's eyes had twinkled. "The nicest. Although I do admit I liked you better in the bath towel."

"Ah." Kyle's eyes met hers with a heat that made her look away. "A woman of taste."

She smiled again now, remembering their earlier shopping trip, but Kyle's expression was grim, a stark contrast to his tuxedo bantering, as he flipped through the papers from his briefcase.

"What are you reading?" she asked.

"Notes from my interviews with Gary Bowen, Dr. Potter, Dr. Kwan and Wayne Pritchard, plus copies of the background checks Court had the Bureau fax to me."

"Anything significant?"

He shook his head and dropped the papers to his lap with a frustrated sigh. "Kwan and Pritchard appear squeaky clean. Dr. Potter had some dubious college activities, but those are ancient history, and he's been free of any un-American associations ever since."

"And Gary's gambling problem?"

"I had a long talk with Gary and his wife yesterday. Gary's joined Gamblers Anonymous and, with the help of a financial counselor, he's consolidated his debts with a loan from a Livingston bank. He's struggling hard to get back on his feet moneywise.

Court's investigation behind the scenes supports what Gary told me. I don't think Bowen's our man.''

Laura frowned. ''That leaves just Lawrence Tyson.''

''The evidence points to him.''

''What evidence?''

Kyle took a deep breath as if gathering his thoughts. For a split second, he looked almost guilty, but that made no sense. His strange expression must have been a trick of the dim lighting inside the plane's cabin.

''When the sheriff was investigating Tyson's disappearance,'' Kyle explained, ''he found some papers in Tyson's desk that indicated he'd been in contact with the Black Order.''

First disbelief, then revulsion at Lawrence's complicity washed through her. Both were quickly replaced by a sudden sadness. The loneliness she'd feared might be coming sooner than she'd expected. ''If Tyson was the informant, then your work at the Institute's done.''

He shook his head. ''It's too neat. On the surface, it looks like Tyson's our man, but I have to dig deeper.''

''But you've just said the rest of the staff are clean.''

''They appear clean.''

''You suspect there's more than one traitor at the Institute? That's preposterous.''

''Think about it,'' Kyle said. ''How could an unknown killer break into the compound and the laboratory, kill Tyson and hide his body without being seen?''

''The same way the terrorists stole the D-5 the first time.''

''Did they?'' His green eyes darkened to almost black, and he rubbed his fingers across the scar that bisected his eyebrow. ''Or did someone on the inside, the same person who killed Tyson, take the D-5 from the lab, hide it, then pass it to the Black Order the next time he or she left the compound?''

Her head ached from the possibilities. ''How will you ever find out?''

''By watching and waiting. If the killer thinks he's in the clear, that Tyson's taken the blame, he may get careless—or cocky. He'll make a mistake. And when he does, I'll be waiting for him.''

Laura shivered at the strength of purpose and ferocity in his face. ''So it's not over.''

He grasped her hand, and the gentleness returned to his expression. ''Sorry, Mrs. Foster, but it looks like you're stuck with me for a while longer.''

Relishing the warmth of his fingers curled around hers, she leaned back against the seat and closed her eyes, fighting back the horror at the suspicion of another traitor—more than a traitor, a murderer—among the staff at the Institute. The only glimpse of a silver lining in that suffocating cloud was that Kyle and Molly would continue to be a part of her life until the killer was caught.

And then what? an inner voice taunted.

And then she was alone again. Completely alone.

THE NEXT EVENING, Kyle snagged a flute of champagne from the tray of a passing waiter and surveyed the spacious gallery of Senator Weston's Georgetown home, filled now with what Molly would dub a flock of tuxedo-clad "pinkwins" and elegant ladies in stunning gowns. Spotting an NBA All-Star, one of Hollywood's leading men and a CNN anchorman, all in the same ridiculous evening wear that Laura had coaxed him into, gave him solace. Misery loved company.

Among the women were nubile young starlets, fashion models and the current hottest country-western singer, but none, however, came close to matching Laura's beauty and style.

Kyle had dressed early in the intimacy of their D.C. hotel suite, then fled to the hotel bar to allow Laura privacy to prepare for the party. After calling Molly, who was delighted to stay with Jewel, Dale and Ribbons at the ranch while he and Laura were in Washington, he ordered a drink. He was nursing his second scotch-on-the-rocks and watching the baseball playoffs when someone tapped him on the shoulder. He'd turned and almost had his socks knocked off.

"Ready?" Laura asked.

For a second, winded by her beauty, he couldn't find his voice. Her floor-length dress of a clinging midnight-blue fabric revealed every luscious curve, and its tiny straps left the creamy skin of her shoulders deliciously bare. She'd piled her hair in curls atop her head, but a few errant ones spilled below her ears and brushed the nape of her neck. Desire stirred deep inside him, a reaction he'd feared had died with his unhappy marriage. Overcome with a sudden and savage urge to kiss each spot those curls touched, he downed the remainder of his drink in one gulp to keep from acting on his impulses.

"Ready." He slid off the bar stool and held out his arm for her. "Since, according to Daniel's orders, I have to attend this high-powered shindig, at least I'll have the enjoyment of escorting the prettiest woman there."

"Why, Dr. Foster." She blushed with pleasure and looped her arm through his. "You do say the nicest things."

"Remember that," he said with a wry grin. "Maybe it will compensate for all the times I'll put my foot in my mouth later tonight. I hate these things. If God had intended me to attend social functions, I'd have been born with a silver tongue in my mouth."

"I've never found you lacking in the conversation department," she said.

"How can you tell?" he asked with a grin. "I'm a man of few words."

"Actions speak louder than words, and I like what you do."

Her blue eyes matched the fabric of her gown, and he was mesmerized by the sparkle of dangling earrings and the tantalizing sight of her bare earlobes. His second drink had gone straight to his head, and if he didn't get himself under control, he might ravish her in the cab on the way to the party. His curiosity piqued.

She'd said she liked what he did. How would she like *that* action?

Calling on the rigid discipline that had guided him in life and work, he inhaled a deep steadying breath that took in the stimulating scent of her orange-blossom perfume. Aware of the admiring glances she drew from the other patrons in the bar, he guided her toward the door. "We don't want to be late."

The cab deposited them before a deceptively small house on a quiet, tree-lined street. With the cobbled walk and Federalist architecture, they could have gone back two centuries in time—except for the security guards carefully checking invitations and the ugly high-tech metal detector they had to pass through at the door.

Kyle also spotted members of the Secret Service contingent who were guarding the presidential candidate. In spite of their immaculately tailored tuxedos, they were hard to miss with their broad shoulders, gazes constantly in motion, earpieces with cords that disappeared into their collars and the barely visible bulk of sidearms beneath their coats.

Kyle and Laura entered the street-level foyer, then climbed a broad, curving staircase to an immense gallery on the second floor. The wide hall, lined with artwork, opened at one end onto a terrace, and the entire area was crowded with people. Among the celebrities and dignitaries, Kyle had easily picked out the other Secret Service members, several of them female.

While Laura had disappeared into the powder room to check her evening wrap, Kyle sipped his

champagne. If he had to be here, he might as well
relax and enjoy himself. For one night, he could forget about hunting down the Black Order. If there
were terrorists around, Weston had enough Secret
Service agents on duty to subdue a small army.

"Having fun?" Laura reappeared at his elbow.

"Like a pig at a barbecue."

"Oh, it's not that bad," she cajoled him. "How
often can you rub elbows with the rich and famous?"

He smiled. "There *are* some interesting folks here.
Usually the interesting people I meet end up behind
bars."

"But this crowd is different."

"Yeah, this crowd can afford bail."

She swatted him playfully on the arm. "Behave."

"Or what?" he whispered in her ear, and resisted
the urge to nibble her lobe. "You'll make me leave?
That would be a treat."

He caught her swift intake of breath and straightened to face the man who'd approached them. Kyle
didn't need an introduction to know who he was. The
senator's face had been plastered on every billboard,
newspaper and television screen for the past year.

"Senator Weston," Laura said. "How nice to see
you again. This is my husband, Kyle Foster."

"Dr. Foster, Laura. So glad you could come."

Kyle studied the man with curiosity. According to
the latest polls, Weston would probably become the
next president of the United States. Several inches
taller than Kyle, the senator sported the physique of
a man who'd once been in spectacular shape but had
obviously sat too long at a desk the past few years.

His brown hair, striped with distinguished touches of gray, set off his George Hamilton tan, and his broad grin displayed teeth too perfect not to be the work of a cosmetic dentist.

But it was Weston's eyes that struck Kyle hardest and created a shiver of distaste in his gut. Weston's sparkling blues seemed friendly enough, but only on the surface. Kyle had the feeling the man could change moods as easily and as quickly as a philanderer switched women. The man was a chameleon, but that was consistent with his career. How could he be an effective politician without being all things to all people?

Experiencing an immediate dislike for the man, Kyle worked to hide it. If he offended the senator, Daniel would have his hide.

"Thanks for inviting us, Senator," he said. "We appreciate the support you've given the Institute."

"And I appreciate the work the Institute is doing for our country," Weston said with more heartiness than sincerity. Both men avoided mentioning the top-secret operation at Montana Confidential, even though Weston sat on the senate committee that oversaw the project. "I'm sure, Laura, that you and Dr. Foster will be able to keep up the good work your father started."

Someone touched the senator's elbow, and he excused himself and turned and moved away.

"How can a man like that be ahead in the polls?" Kyle muttered. "He's a first-class fake."

"People are afraid," Laura said, "especially since

the Montana capitol bombing. They want someone who promises it won't happen again.''

"No one can promise that," Kyle said. "It's a mean world out there."

Laura shuddered. "You're preaching to the choir."

Kyle felt a sudden kick of guilt. "Hey, you look fantastic and you're supposed to be having a good time. Let's find you some champagne and mingle."

On the terrace, they found a table stocked with champagne and canapes. Kyle handed Laura a glass and was loading a plate with crab puffs when Governor Haskel stepped out of the crowd and approached them.

"Hello, Governor," Laura said with an ease and grace that Kyle found admirable. "It's good to see you again."

She introduced Kyle, and he shook the governor's hand, noting the man looked tired and distracted.

"You're looking radiant," Haskel said to Laura. "Marriage must agree with you. And you, Foster, you're a lucky man."

"Yes, sir."

"How are you feeling, Governor?" Laura asked. "Have you recovered from your injuries?"

Haskel's shoulders slumped, and he shook his head. "The body heals, but the spirit—I don't like living in a world where innocent people suffer and die at the hands of fanatics."

Kyle lifted his champagne glass. "I'll drink to that."

"Do you think Senator Weston's the man who can stop the terrorists?" Laura asked.

"If he can't," the governor said, "God help us all."

An older woman called to him, and the governor said goodbye and joined her.

"Poor man," Laura said. "He feels terrible about what's happened in his state."

"He's one of the few who know about the D-5 and anthrax. Like the rest of us, he's probably waiting for the other shoe to drop."

Kyle spotted a Secret Service agent standing on the threshold of the French doors and scanning the crowd, his expression grim. When he located Kyle and Laura, he strode toward them.

"Dr. Foster?" the agent asked.

"Yes."

"Will you come with me, please?"

"Something wrong?"

"Just follow me, please, sir. I'll explain later."

With alarm bells screaming in his brain, Kyle took Laura's arm and trailed in the wake of the agent who cut through the crowd like an armored tank through a canebrake. They passed quickly through the gallery and then a side door that led to a butler's pantry. There the agent turned to face them.

"What's up?" Kyle demanded.

"Senator Weston said you could help, sir. We've found a bomb in the kitchen. It could blow any minute."

Chapter Eleven

"We're evacuating the residence and adjoining houses in a four-block radius," the agent said. "The bomb squad's on the way."

Emotions swarmed at Kyle like a cloud of killer bees.

Anger at the terrorists.

Concern for Weston's guests.

Fear of his own inadequacy in disarming the bomb, a terror so deep it brought a cold sweat to his forehead.

Love for Molly.

Love for Laura.

Laura. Just the thought of her gave him strength. He drew on discipline and experience, and calm settled around him like a cloaking fog, steadying his hands, steeling his purpose. Looking at Laura, he snapped to the agent, "Get her out of here."

"No." Panic sparked in her magnificent eyes, and she grasped his sleeve. "The bomb squad's coming. Let them handle this. Come with me."

With a rueful smile, he gently pried her fingers

from his arm. "Go. The squad may not get here in time. I have to do this."

Without a further word, she flung her arms around his neck and kissed him hard on the lips with a violence that almost knocked him over. "I love you," he heard her whisper before she broke free. She ran from the room without a backward look before he could respond.

"This way, sir." The agent held open the swinging door to the kitchen, and Kyle preceded him into the now-deserted room. His attention was drawn immediately to the open cabinet doors beneath the sink. A massive box with ominous blinking lights was attached to the drainpipe.

Kyle stripped off his jacket and began rolling up his sleeves. "Get me a screwdriver, some wirecutters and a flashlight."

The agent took off at a run.

Concentrating on the task at hand to maintain his composure, Kyle eased to a cross-legged position on the floor and studied the bomb. "This has Black Order written all over it," he muttered. His voice echoed eerily in the empty room.

He leaned forward, and with precise and careful movements, slowly peeled back a piece of duct tape. Beneath the sticky residue the digits on the timer blinked like a countdown to eternity.

Six minutes and counting.

For an instant, his calm slipped and his hands trembled when he realized that so much tape covered the box, it might take him longer than six minutes to expose the detonator. His next discovery made his blood run cold. He shivered involuntarily and cursed in the silence.

The duct tape enveloped enough C-4 explosive to take down a city block.

Footsteps sounded behind him, and someone thrust tools into his hands. "I'll hold the flashlight for you, sir," the returning agent said.

Kyle turned to the agent with the young and eager face, just like Buzz Williams's had been. In vivid flashback, Kyle's mind replayed the horror of his former partner's last moments when the bomb he'd been deactivating at the Hollywood Bowl exploded prematurely.

"No need," Kyle said gruffly. "Just set the light on a chair so it illuminates the bomb and get the hell out of here."

The agent squatted beside him and held the flashlight steady. "You may need help."

"I can handle it. You didn't sign on for this."

"With all due respect, sir, neither did you."

Kyle paused from carefully peeling away the duct tape and glanced at the young man at his side. His demeanor was calm, his hands steady, but Kyle could read the fear in his gray eyes.

Kyle nodded in grim acceptance. "Cut the *sir* crap. Call me Kyle."

"Yes, si—, Kyle. I'm Jason."

"Okay, Jason, keep the light steady."

"You've done this before?"

"Not this particular kind of bomb—"

Jason groaned. "Please, tell me you can do this."

"I'm trained in bomb disposal," he assured the

young agent with more confidence than he felt, and thrust the awful memories of Buzz's final moments from his mind. "I know what I'm doing."

Beside him, Jason grinned. "Good thing one of us does, anyway."

With slow, deliberate movements that made the muscles in his shoulders scream with pain, Kyle continued to strip away tape. He had to expose the wires leading from the timer to the detonator and cut them before the C-4 blew.

Four minutes.

Sweat poured into his eyes and stuck his shirt to his skin. He wanted to hurry, but he had to proceed carefully. One false move, release the wrong strip of securing tape, and the bomb could drop from the drainpipe. That impact could short-circuit the timer and blow him, Jason and a sizable chunk of Georgetown to kingdom come.

He could hear Jason's tortured breathing beside him, matching his own, but the beam of the flashlight never wavered.

Two minutes.

"I'm in," Kyle said with a whoosh of relief. "Now all I have to do is clip the wire. Hand me the cutters."

Jason passed him the tool. "How do you know which one to cut?"

"They're color-coded."

"That's good."

"Yeah," Kyle said with a grimace. "Unless the bastards purposely switched the wires to throw us off."

"What are you going to do?" The hitch of fear in Jason's voice was impossible to miss.

One minute.

Kyle pointed to the innards of the bomb. "I'm going to cut that wire and pray. It's been nice knowing you, Jason."

For a fleeting instant, he conjured an image of Laura, blue eyes shining, black hair dancing in the wind, and an alluring smile upon her eminently kissable lips. Her parting declaration of love echoed in his mind.

Then with a steady hand and a sinking heart, Kyle snipped the lead to the detonator.

A FEW MILES AWAY and a half hour later, Laura paced the aisle of the church where the party-goers and Weston's neighbors had gathered after the evacuation. The crowd had thinned as Weston's guests had been picked up by their limousines, but the church was still packed, some people in evening clothes, others in pajamas and hastily donned robes and slippers.

In the narthex, surrounded by a shouting mob of reporters and the blinding glare of television cameras, Weston was issuing a statement to the media. Newsmen and -women elbowed one another for an opportunity to fling their questions at the senator, who answered with the cool aplomb of a politician accustomed to the media barrage.

Grouped on the pews in the sanctuary, evacuees talked softly among themselves, ashen and shaken at being rousted from their homes. Red Cross workers moved among them, dispensing coffee, soft drinks, doughnuts and consolation. Laura, however, couldn't sit still. As she paced, she listened, constantly braced for the rumble of the explosion, the concussion of a blast that she recalled from her own horrible experience would be felt even this far away.

She had faith in Kyle's expertise, but she also knew the Black Order's treachery. Her father hadn't survived their bomb. She could only pray fervently that Kyle would. Terrified as she had been of another explosion, she'd wanted to stay with him, even if remaining meant they'd die together. Weeks before, she'd lost her father, the only family she'd had. Then Kyle had entered her life, and, to her surprise, she'd learned to love again, despite her grief, despite the scars Curt had left on her heart and her ego.

She groaned inwardly, remembering how tightly she'd clung to Kyle at the senator's place. She should never had told him she loved him before she raced from the house. Maybe he'd forget her brashness in the chaos that followed. Otherwise, living with him and pretending she'd never admitted her feelings was going to be awkward, uncomfortable. But, oh dear God, she hoped she'd have that chance.

He isn't going to die, she promised herself.

But she was going to lose him anyway. Even if he outwitted the terrorist bomb, once the Black Order had been apprehended, Kyle would walk out of her life forever. And take Molly with him.

Molly! How could she ever explain to that adorable child if anything happened to her daddy?

That traumatic thought quickened her steps until

her pacing became frenetic. A firm hand on her elbow dragged her to a halt.

"Mrs. Foster."

She turned to find Senator Weston, his handsome
face etched with concern, his eyes sympathetic,
standing in the aisle.

"Have you heard something?" she begged. "Is
Kyle all right?"

He shook his head sadly. "No news. The bomb
squad arrived. They're sweeping the house. It could
be a long night. I've asked my driver to take you
back to your hotel."

"But—"

"You'll be more comfortable there." Ross Weston's expression was kind but firm. "And I'm sure
Dr. Foster will want to return there to rest as soon
as this ordeal is over."

She started to protest again, but realized the senator was right. She allowed him to steer her through
the throng of reporters, still tossing questions at him,
and into the luxurious limo. His cadre of Secret Service agents hovered in the background, alert and on
guard.

"Don't worry," he assured her. "I'm sure everything will turn out fine."

"Thank you." Her eyes teared with emotion that
the senator exhibited so much concern for her welfare, when he was the terrorists' target.

She leaned back in the seat as the car pulled away
from the church, away from the neighborhood where
Kyle remained face-to-face with a Black Order
bomb. The senator's optimism had been kind but

misguided. She had witnessed firsthand the thoroughness of the terrorists' hatred, the devastation of their rage. She closed her eyes and prayed for a miracle.

HOURS LATER, on the sofa in the hotel suite, stripped of her party dress and wrapped in a warm robe, Laura sat glued to the local news channel. Television cameras had not been allowed near Senator Weston's house, but with telephoto and night-vision lenses, they telecast fuzzy shots of the mansion surrounded by police cars, members of the bomb squad coming and going and the cumbersome bomb-disposal truck.

No sign of Kyle.

"The search continues for terrorist bombs in the Georgetown home of Senator Ross Weston," the anchorwoman's flawless voice droned over the live shots. "Apparently, with Senator Weston far ahead in the polls for next month's presidential election, the terrorists are taking exception to his tough antiterrorism platform. Tonight's bombing effort is seen as a direct strike against Weston's stance, possibly even an attempt to kill the senator before the election. As a result, the entire capital is on a high state of alert...."

Laura scanned the blurred green images until her eyes ached. All she wanted was one glimpse of Kyle to assure her he was all right.

While she watched, she bargained with herself. If Kyle survived this bombing attempt, she would place herself on her best behavior. She'd play the part of Mrs. Kyle Foster as convincingly as she could, but she'd remember to hold her heart in check, her emotions in reserve. She wouldn't embarrass him again as she had by flinging herself at him in the senator's butler's pantry with pronouncements of love. And she'd protect her own heart from being smashed to smithereens, so that when Kyle and Molly walked out of her life forever, she wouldn't shed a tear.

Repeating her silent mantra, she stared at the television and prayed for a glimpse of Kyle. The next thing she knew, dim light filtered through the open draperies, the dawn sky above the Potomac had turned a soft pink and someone was shaking her shoulder.

Still groggy from sleep, she looked up into a pair of deep sea-green eyes smiling down at her. Joy and relief cascaded through her, scouring away every earlier promise of self-control and self-denial she had affirmed so vehemently before falling asleep. Nothing else mattered now. Not her pride, not visions of her lonely future. All that mattered was that Kyle was alive, whole and well.

And she loved him.

"Kyle!" She bolted upright, straight into his arms.

He pulled her against him and buried his face in her hair. "God, it's been a hell of a night."

She pulled back and scanned his face, etched with fine lines of fatigue. "You okay?"

"I am now."

Recalling too late her recent vow to keep her distance, she started to pull away, but he hugged her tighter.

"I wasn't afraid, Laura." His lips moved against

her ear. "I thought I would be, especially after what happened to Buzz. But the whole time I was disarming that damn contraption, all I could think of was you and Molly. I wasn't going to let the Black Order's bomb keep me from you."

He was delirious, she told herself. Drunk with fatigue, strung out from tension. He couldn't mean what he was saying. And if she gave in to her impulses now, she'd be sure to regret it. The prospect of leaving him was already hard enough, but if she caved in to his hallucinations and made love with him, their ultimate parting would be all the more painful.

She placed her hands against the broad expanse of his chest and pushed away. He released her slightly, enough to peer down into her eyes, but held her fast in his embrace.

"You're exhausted," she said. "You need a hot shower and a long rest."

"Eventually." His eyes were like green smoke. "But right now, what I need is you."

Discouraging him was one of the hardest things she'd ever had to do. Her heart, every nerve in her body screamed in protest.

"It isn't me you want," she insisted with a casualness she didn't feel. "Your body simply needs a release from the stress you've been through."

Her words must have shocked him, because he dropped his arms from around her, and she almost stumbled at his release. With a savage jerk, he stripped off his tuxedo jacket and tossed it across a chair.

"Is that what you really think?" His deep, rich voice was sharp-edged with anger. "That I'd use you as a quickie stress-buster?"

She swallowed hard. He was more handsome than ever when angry. She wanted him to love her. To make love to her. But when—if—that ever happened, she wanted it to be for real, not the result of battle fatigue.

"I think you're an honorable man." She damned the quiver of emotion in her voice and tried to steady her tone. "Right now you believe you want me, but you've been up all night, risking your life. How can you be certain your desire isn't just post-traumatic stress, your body telling your head you need physical relief?"

He smiled, a slow and easy upturn of his lips that turned her knees to Jell-O. "Because I've wanted you since you walked into the bar last night looking like a knockout in that blue dress."

She held her head high. "Wanting and loving are two different things. I don't believe in casual sex."

"Neither do I."

With a sharp intake of breath, she tried to calm her whirling senses. "What are you saying?"

He moved toward her again and wrapped her in a gentle embrace. "That I love you, *Mrs. Foster.*" His eyebrows lifted with his wicked grin. "And, if I remember your words from last night correctly, you love me."

His strong, capable hands, moving in mesmerizing circles on her back, made it hard for her to think, and his words had knocked what little air was left from her lungs.

"You love me?"

"More every day. I didn't realize how much until I faced that bomb and the fact that I might never see you again."

He lowered his lips and barely brushed hers, sending a shower of sparks along her nerves, detonating a tremor of need, making her long for more.

Threading his fingers through her hair, he tilted her face until their gazes locked. "Tell me you don't love me, Laura. Tell me you don't want me as much as I want you, and I'll let you go. I'll walk into that bathroom, take a shower and walk out as if nothing's happened, and we'll go back to our charade, our pretend marriage."

"I don't—"

His eyes darkened with pain. He relinquished her and stepped back.

She moved closer to him and traced his strong jaw with her fingers, eased her thumb over the scar across his eyebrow. "Don't jump to conclusions. I was about to say I don't know how I can be so lucky."

With a whoop of joy, he crushed her in his arms, lifted her off her feet and whirled her around the room. The hem of her robe swept his folders on the Black Order from the desk, but Kyle didn't seem to notice. Abruptly, he set her down and studied her face, his own suddenly serious.

"You're sure?" he asked.

She nodded. "I've loved you from the moment you appeared in the capitol that awful day."

With a groan, he claimed her lips again. Passion exploded within her in response to his fiery kiss. She forced her hands between them and fumbled with the buttons on his shirt. He reached for the knotted sash of her robe, but it refused to disengage.

"Damn," he muttered. "These fingers can disarm a bomb, but they're helpless now."

Taking pity on his impatience, an eagerness that mirrored her own, she quickly untied the sash. It dropped to the floor, and her robe billowed open, revealing her nakedness.

Kyle pushed the garment from her shoulders, and it puddled at her feet.

"God, you're even more beautiful than I'd imagined." His voice was stunned, awe-filled.

He scooped her into his arms and carried her to the king-size bed. After depositing her among the pillows, he swiftly shed his own clothes and lay beside her. She reveled in the warmth of his skin against hers. Sliding her fingers over the scars on his chest, she kissed the reminders of how close he'd come once before to losing his life.

He gripped her to him, and she buried her face against his shoulder. "I was so scared tonight."

"Scared?"

"Afraid you wouldn't make it. I can't imagine life without you."

He shifted above her and gazed down with smoldering eyes. "You're sure you want to go through with this?"

"This?"

He ran his fingers lazily down her breasts, across

her stomach, between her thighs, and she shivered in anticipation.

"If we consummate this marriage," he said teasingly, "an annulment's out. You'll be stuck with me."

She arched against him, wanting more, and flashed him a wanton smile. "I can stand staying married if you can."

"You're sure?" His lips teased her nipples.

She gasped with pleasure. "You certainly know how to set off explosives."

He grinned. "Just doing my job, ma'am." His lips continued their exploration.

She struggled for breath. "And you're damn good at what you do."

"I aim to please." He nibbled at her earlobe.

"Please—"

His green eyes glowed with desire and a hint of amusement. "Please, what?"

"Love me."

"Oh, I do, Mrs. Foster. Without a doubt."

"Show me."

He entered her with surprising tenderness, molding his body to hers, and the heat of his passion quickly filled her until she felt they had stumbled into a consuming inferno of desire. Every nerve in her body kindled with delight and forged her to him on a cellular level, their flesh one. As he stoked the fire higher, his gaze, like green flames, held hers, and his lips murmured her name. Too soon, the explosion came, a flash of star-flung fireworks, plunging them both over the edge in a conflagration of breathless pleasure.

Afterward, she had only a moment to lie sated and content before he rose and tugged her into the suite's bathroom. They made slow, languid love in the immense whirlpool bath, and remained tangled comfortably in each other's arms until the water began to cool.

With reluctance, she stepped from the tub, toweled dry and slipped on her robe.

"Hungry?" she asked.

"Famished." His expression had nothing to do with food, and he reached for her again. Reluctantly, knowing he needed food and rest, she eluded his grasp.

"I'll order breakfast." Happier than she could ever remember, Laura leaned down and kissed him.

He clasped her face between his large, gentle hands. "No regrets."

"Just one," she replied, straight-faced.

His expression darkened. "What?"

"That we didn't do this days ago." She scurried from the room to avoid the water he splashed at her.

Kyle's file on the Black Order lay scattered across the floor in front of the desk. On her way to phone room service, she scooped up the papers and was stuffing them back in the folder when a name caught her eye. Dropping into the desk chair, she began to read. Her eyes widened in shock and betrayal.

Minutes later, when Kyle came out of the bathroom, wearing only a towel and a cocky grin, she turned on him. "How dare you!"

Her icy words stopped him in his tracks. "What's wrong?" he asked.

"Where did you get these papers?"

The telephone on the desk rang, and Kyle moved to answer it.

"Leave it," Laura snapped. "Whoever it is can wait."

Her heart was breaking, and only the fire of her anger kept her from bursting into tears. Kyle looked so deliciously handsome, he'd made love to her with a fierce tenderness unlike anything she'd ever experienced, and he'd been deceiving her all along.

Ignoring the ringing phone, she picked up the offensive documents and waved them in her fist. "Where did these come from?"

He approached her, his demeanor stern, and took the papers she had brandished like a weapon in his face.

"They were found in Lawrence Tyson's desk," he said after skimming through them.

After numerous rings, the phone fell silent.

"They're lies." Her entire body vibrated with rage. "My father *never* had any connection to the Black Order."

With his broad back to her, he replaced the papers in the folder. "It's my job to prove whether he did or didn't." His voice was low, its tone controlled.

"The Black Order blew my father to bits, and now *you*—" she sputtered, grappling for words through a red curtain of rage "—you have the audacity to imply he was involved with these killers. It's like killing him all over again."

"I'm not implying anything," he said calmly. "I'm only studying the evidence."

She wanted to hit him, throw something at him, hurt him as he'd hurt her. "You believe my father's a traitor, you're working to convict him, to ruin his good name—all of him that's left—and yet you made love to me?"

"It doesn't matter—"

She stared in horror. "You honestly think it doesn't matter to me that you're accusing my father?"

Shaking his head, he turned from the desk to face her. "Your father's guilt or innocence has nothing to do with how I feel about you."

She clasped her hands to her temples, afraid her head would explode from the conflicting emotions swelling in her brain. "I can't love a man who's out to destroy my father."

"I'm not out to destroy anyone—"

The phone shrilled insistently on the desk, and Kyle cast her an apologetic look. "I have to answer that. It could be important."

"Go ahead." Her heartbreak was overpowering her anger, and she struggled not to cry. "There's nothing more for us to talk about."

Kyle looked as if he wanted to say more, but the phone continued its annoying interruption. He grabbed the receiver.

"Foster here."

Overwhelmed with sadness, Laura watched his expression turn from irritation to alarm as he listened to the person on the other end of the line.

"When?" His query split the air like a thunder-clap, making Laura jump. Then he fell silent while the caller talked.

Laura watched in bewilderment as his face paled beneath his healthy Montana tan. From his strained, shocked reaction, she realized something terrible had happened.

"We'll catch the first plane back." Kyle hung up the phone and turned to her, his face dark with rage and despair.

Fear caught in her throat, and she forced herself to speak through wooden lips. "Molly?"

Kyle's face softened fleetingly at his daughter's name. "Molly's fine."

"Then what's wrong?"

"It's Governor Haskel. He was taken from his ho-tel during the night."

"Kidnapped?"

Kyle nodded grimly. "By the Black Order."

"But he's been under extra security guard since the bombing."

"The terrorists infiltrated the hotel staff. His entire team was found drugged. A powerful sedative in the coffee delivered by room service."

Her anger at Kyle momentarily forgotten, Laura remembered how kind the governor had been to her after her father's death. "What will they do to him?"

"They're demanding a ransom for his return."

"Oh, no." Laura's knees gave way and she col-lapsed into a chair.

"But that's not the worst," Kyle continued.

Laura shook her head. "What could be worse?"

''If the ransom isn't paid and the Black Order members now being held by authorities aren't released within forty-eight hours, the terrorists have promised to deposit the D-5 in the water supply of a Montana city.''

Chapter Twelve

Kyle felt as if he'd been ripped down the middle. Part of him wanted to draw Laura into his arms, to assure her he'd do everything he could to clear her father's name, but the cop in him knew he had a job to do. Personal feelings would have to wait. Thousands of lives were at stake.

"That was Daniel on the phone," he explained. "Foiling the Black Order's attempt at the senator's house last night apparently didn't sit well with them. They want revenge."

Her eyes teared. "How many more innocent lives do these murderers need before they're satisfied?"

"Daniel wants us to fly home immediately." Kyle chose his words carefully. Laura wasn't going to like what he had to say. "He still believes the key to locating the terrorists is at the Institute."

"Of course." Her anger vanished, along with her tears, replaced by an icy reserve. "I'll pack."

Hours later, in the sky over the Midwest, Laura still hadn't defrosted. Her manner was painstakingly polite, Kyle thought with a sigh of regret, but he'd need the plane's deicers to find a trace of the warmth and passion they'd shared earlier that morning.

When he withdrew the Institute's personnel files from his briefcase for further study, he caught her sharp intake of breath.

"Something wrong?" He knew the answer, but hoped by talking he could ease the tension between them.

"I demand you return those," she stated in a low but savage voice, "and ban you from ever stepping foot on the Institute compound again."

With a sinking heart, he shrugged. Their conversation hadn't taken the turn he'd hoped for. "Then I'll have to procure a search warrant to have legal access to the complex to recover them."

With an imperious tilt of her head and the wintry glint of her magnificent blue eyes, she was more beautiful than ever. And completely untouchable. Deep down, he'd known she'd react this way to any suspicion cast on her father. That's why he'd been so careful to hide it. But facts were facts. Eventually, she would have to face the truth.

"Laura," he said in his most reasonable tone, appealing to her better nature, "I didn't *plant* the evidence against your father. I'm just the messenger. How long are you going to hold that against me?"

"That's it!" Her eyes lost their icy glare and blazed with excitement. "That folder that implicates Daddy. It was planted."

Kyle groaned inwardly and shook his head. "You don't know that."

She grasped his arm, her slender fingers and beautifully manicured nails biting into his skin. "Think about it. Lawrence Tyson wasn't a stupid man. In fact, like Daddy and Dr. Potter, he had a brilliant mind. Why would he have left such incriminating documents unsecured in his desk where anyone could find them?"

"Maybe he didn't expect to be murdered." Kyle couldn't keep the irony from his voice.

"Or maybe, like you speculated before, the real terrorist informer *killed* him *and* planted the incriminating documents to steer suspicion away from himself."

"You have a point. But if someone did plant the file, the question is who? Here, you take Melinda Kwan's folder and I'll take Wayne Pritchard's. See if you can find anything questionable in her background."

Laura frowned. "Why these two? I thought you said they're both squeaky clean."

"Maybe too clean. If you falsified your background, wouldn't you be tempted to make it perfect?"

For the next hour, Kyle read and reread Pritchard's file. Something buried in the pages of information niggled at the back of his mind, but he couldn't put his finger on it.

Beside him, Laura closed Dr. Kwan's folder. "I've studied this upside down and backward. If the woman is hiding anything, my eyes can't find it."

"*Eyes!* That's what I've been missing." Kyle turned to her in his excitement as the pieces fell into place. She'd solved the puzzle. More than anything,

he wanted to kiss her, but feared a bad case of frost-
bite if he tried.

"What are you talking about?" The smooth perfection of Laura's high forehead crinkled in puzzle-
ment, and he resisted the impulse to even the silky
contour with his thumb.

"Eyes," he said. "That's the key. What color are
Wayne Pritchard's eyes?"

"Brown," she replied without hesitation. "I remember because they always remind me of dirty ice,
just like my former husband's. So what?"

"Because on Pritchard's first driver's license application, issued when he was sixteen, his eyes are
described as hazel."

She shook her head. "You're grasping at straws.
Hazel eyes are sometimes more brown, sometimes
more greenish."

"That's true, but my gut tells me I'm on the right
track. Pritchard's been very helpful in the investigation. Almost too helpful." He pulled his cell phone
from his pocket and punched in the number for the
ranch. "I'll have Court and the FBI do a deeper
background check, all the way back to the cradle,
just to make certain we haven't missed anything."

When Daniel came on the line, Kyle filled in his
boss on his suspicions and told him what he needed
from Court and the FBI.

"Does this mean Daddy's in the clear?" she asked
when Kyle broke the connection. The hopefulness in
her expression wrenched at his heart.

"Not yet. We have to verify the origin of those
incriminating documents first."

"I don't need verification. I *know* he's innocent." The acid in her tone could have etched steel.

"I admire your loyalty, but I've got to have more than that to go on."

"Fine." The acid turned to ice, a glacial anger that froze his hopes. "Just finish your investigation quickly so we can end this ridiculous sham of a marriage as soon as possible."

Mourning the loss of the intimacy they'd shared earlier and his dreams of making a family with Laura, he let his disappointment boil into anger. "We'll work quickly all right. In case you've forgotten, there's more at stake than your father's honor. The lives of Governor Haskel and thousands of others are on the line."

She flushed with embarrassment, but he could tell her fury hadn't dissipated. They spent the remainder of the flight and the long drive back to the Institute in strained silence.

When they arrived at the house, Laura hurried upstairs, then reappeared a few minutes later. She'd changed into jeans, a sweater and low-heeled boots.

"Going out?" he asked.

"There's work to catch up on at the lab."

"I can't go with you. I have to wait for Court's call."

"I'll be fine. The place is crawling with security, remember?"

He wanted to grab her and kiss some sense into her, but the rigid set of her shoulders and the haughty angle of her chin warned him off.

Suddenly the ice in her eyes softened. "What about Molly?"

She loved his daughter. He could see it in her face. Then why the hell couldn't she love him, too? Especially since she knew by investigating her father he was just doing his job.

"She'll stay at the ranch for now. It's safer."

Disappointment flickered across her exquisite features, and without another word, she turned and hurried out the door.

Kyle let out a stream of curses. How had he managed to screw things up so royally? Everything had been so perfect earlier this morning, but her unshakable loyalty to Josiah had spoiled all that. Somehow Laura had convinced herself that she had to choose between him and her father, and in that contest, even with Molly on his side, he didn't stand a chance.

He had started up the stairs to unpack his bag, when the phone rang. He turned and rushed to Josiah's den to answer it.

"You were right," Court's voice sounded in his ear. "We did a deep background search on Wayne Pritchard."

"And?"

"He died at age sixteen in a car crash."

"Then who the hell is working at the Institute?"

"We sent Pritchard's current prints to Interpol—"

"Let me guess," Kyle interrupted. "He's Agarese."

"Bingo. Born and raised in the Emirate of Agar. Frank's warming up the chopper. We're on our way."

"Meet me at the lab."

Kyle slammed down the phone and raced from the room. His bag remained on the foyer floor where he'd left it. After flinging it open, he removed his automatic, rammed in the clip and activated the slide, loading a bullet in the chamber. Shoving the gun in the waist of his jeans at the small of his back, he headed for the door.

Before he left the house, he calmed himself with a series of deep breaths. He couldn't let Pritchard see him agitated. He wanted to take the bastard by surprise.

Although every muscle in his body and every cell in his brain urged him to hurry, Kyle ambled at a leisurely pace down the road that led from the house to the laboratory.

LAURA SAT BEHIND her father's desk in his office at the laboratory building and struggled not to cry. In the small dark hours of the previous night, while Kyle had faced the terrorist bomb, she had finally admitted that she'd fallen helplessly, hopelessly and irretrievably in love with him. When he'd returned her feelings and made love to her with a passion that took her breath and left her weak with pleasure, she'd feared she'd die of happiness.

Now she was afraid she'd die of misery.

What cut to her core was not just Kyle's accusations against her father but that he had hidden them from her. If Josiah had been simply one of many suspects on Kyle's long list, surely he wouldn't have gone to such lengths to keep his suspicions secret. He truly believed her father guilty.

He believes everyone's *guilty for now,* a tiny voice niggled in her ear. *He even suspects Wayne Pritchard because someone got his eye color wrong on an old application.*

Emotionally exhausted, she shook away her conflicting feelings and refused to think about Kyle for now. The stacks of paperwork on her father's desk, too long neglected, needed her immediate attention.

A few minutes later, she strode down the hall. Through the glass door of the staff lounge, she spotted Dr. Potter, Dr. Kwan, Gary Bowen and C.J. gathered around a table for their afternoon break. The aroma of freshly brewed coffee permeated the room, and Bowen was munching a pastry the size of a Frisbee.

"Grab a cup and join us," C.J. called when Laura entered the room. "Tell us about the excitement in Washington."

"Can't," Laura said with an apologetic shrug. "I'm looking for Wayne. There's a discrepancy on this supply requisition I need clarified right away."

"He was working in Lab One a few minutes ago," Dr. Potter said, "but he's probably already left."

"Left?" Laura asked. "It's only three o'clock."

Potter flashed his congenial smile, an affectionate expression that usually lifted her spirits, but today Laura felt too low to respond. "Said he had a headache," Potter explained, "and was going home early."

"I'll see if I can catch him." Laura slipped out

the door and headed down the long hall toward Lab One at the other end of the building. Her low-heeled boots made no sound on the cushioned vinyl flooring. When the laboratory building had been designed, her dad insisted his scientists have optimum quiet in order to concentrate on their work.

She entered the wide double doors to Lab One, a huge room with cheerful sunlight pouring in the southern wall of glass, efficient rows of shelves and counters on the other three sides. Microscopes, centrifuges and a myriad of the latest scientific equipment, including small isolation chambers accessible only by impermeable latex gloves, covered the stainless steel-topped island that ran down the center of the room.

No sign of Wayne Pritchard.

She was turning to leave, when Wayne suddenly straightened behind the end of an island by the undercounter refrigerator where the scientists stored working samples. Unaware of her presence, he slipped a vial into the pocket of his lab coat and started toward the door. When he spotted her, he stopped, his expression a mixture of guilt and surprise.

"Laura, I thought you were in Washington."

"We came back early. What's in your pocket?" The hair on the back of her neck rose. Was Wayne leaving the lab with a sample? Was *he* their traitor?

With apparent nonchalance, he pulled the vial from his coat and placed it on the counter. "It's a sample of a new strain of D-5."

"A new strain?"

"D-5A. An airborne version of the virus. Dr. Potter asked me to prepare a few slides for some tests he's ready to run on the antidote C.J.'s working on."

"I thought you had a headache."

He smiled, flashing a handsome grin that didn't quite reach his eyes. "Took some aspirin. I'm fine now. You wanted to see me about something?"

She handed him the requisition form. "Your request for petrie dishes. The writing's smudged and I can't make out the quantity. Is that a two or a seven?"

He glanced at the sheet and handed it back to her. "A seven. One hundred and seventy-five."

He seemed edgy, not his usual self. Curious, she moved a little closer, trying for a better look at his eyes. "You like working here?"

"You bet. The staff are like family." In spite of his apparent nervousness, he met her gaze head-on.

His irises were a deep, murky brown, just as she'd remembered, but today she noted something else reflected there. Cold, menacing malice. An involuntary shiver shook her body.

"Something wrong?" he asked.

Afraid she'd given her suspicions away, she shook her head. "The air conditioning's always too cold in the labs."

He narrowed his eyes. "You were looking at me funny, like you'd never seen me before."

"I was just thinking about your comment on family. We've lost two of our staff in the past month. I'm having trouble coming to terms with their deaths."

"We all are." His declaration rang false. "Anything else? I really need to get to work on these slides. Dr. Potter's expecting them."

"He thinks you've gone home."

"Then he'll be pleasantly surprised."

KYLE REACHED the lab building and stopped at the reception desk. "Is Wayne Pritchard still in the building?"

The security guard checked his roster. "He hasn't signed out yet. Most of the staff meets in the lounge this time of the afternoon for a coffee break. You'll probably find him there."

Kyle hurried to the lounge. He found the entire staff assembled around a table—all except Pritchard.

"Anyone know where Wayne is?" Kyle asked.

"He said he was going home with a headache," Dr. Potter said.

Kyle shook his head. "He hasn't signed out with security."

"Find Laura and she can probably tell you," C.J. said. "She was in here just minutes ago looking for him, too."

"Last time I saw him," Potter added, "he was working in Lab One."

"Thanks." Kyle, heart pounding with apprehension, left the lounge and strode down the corridor toward the lab. He hoped Laura hadn't found Pritchard. His confrontation with the terrorist wasn't going to be friendly, and the last thing Kyle wanted was Laura caught in the crossfire.

He swung open the doors to Lab One. In the center

of the long, narrow room Laura stood beside Pritchard. Her eyes widened with surprise when she spotted Kyle in the doorway.

"Are you looking for me?"

"Yeah," Kyle lied. "There's a phone call for you. You'd better take it in the office."

Laura started toward him, but Wayne grabbed her and jerked her back. Kyle wanted to rush him, but he noted the angle of Wayne's hold. With his arm around her throat, the slightest increase in pressure could crush her windpipe.

"What the hell are you doing, Pritchard?" Kyle fought to keep calm and pretend surprise. "Is this some kind of joke? Let my wife go."

"Wife! Don't make me laugh." Wayne's face contorted in a snarl. "She's no more your wife than you're a research scientist. You're a cop. And she's my ticket out of here."

"What makes you think I'm after you?" Kyle asked reasonably. "Have you done something you shouldn't?"

"Don't play games with me, Foster. You know who I am. Laura should never play poker. Her suspicions were written all over her face."

Kyle tamped down his fear. He wanted Pritchard in custody, but first he wanted Laura safe. The color had bled from her complexion, and her blue eyes had darkened with fear, but courage was evident in the tilt of her head and the set of her jaw. He caught her gaze and tried to reassure her with his eyes.

"Laura's done nothing to harm you," he said to Wayne. "Let her go. Take me hostage instead."

Kyle's mind was working a mile a minute. There was a leak in the agency. Somehow Wayne knew about Kyle's background and the pretend marriage. But Kyle doubted the terrorist knew about the helicopter full of Montana Confidential agents who'd be landing at the Institute within minutes, waiting for him when he left the building. If Kyle could persuade Wayne to exchange Laura for himself, he could use his hand-to-hand combat skills to take him down once Laura was a safe distance away.

Wayne seemed to read his mind. "You're a trained fighter, Foster. Laura suits my purposes better."

In a lightning move, Kyle reached behind him and whipped out his gun. "I'm also an expert marksman. I can put a bullet between your eyes before you take another breath. Now let her go."

Wayne swung Laura to cover his face, and at his sudden movement, the sleeve of his lab coat swept a vial from the countertop. It crashed to the floor and shattered, sending a pale gold liquid splattering across the floor, the counter and over Laura's feet.

Wayne's face paled, and he cursed in Arabic, but he didn't lessen his grip on Laura's throat. Laura stared at Kyle in panic.

"What was in the vial?" Kyle asked. He could tell from her expression something terrible had just been released.

"D-5A," Laura said. "An airborne virus. You might as well let me go, Wayne. We're all dead anyway."

Chapter Thirteen

Immediately, Kyle reached to the wall beside him and hit the large red panic button, one of six scattered around the room. A Klaxon blared throughout the building, its high-pitched screech jolting Kyle to the bone. Within seconds, a huge shutter descended over the window, blocking out the sun and preventing the virus from escaping to the outside. Above him, the ventilation system shifted into high gear, and he heard the reassuring whir of scrubbers, sucking the air from the room to disinfect it.

But the scrubbers were too late to help Laura. Too late to help any of them.

"Let her go," Kyle ordered Wayne, who still held Laura in a stranglehold. "None of us is going anywhere with the lab locked down, and she's no protection to you now."

Pritchard dropped his arm from around Laura's neck and raced to a sink at the end of the lab. With frantic motions, he peeled off his shoes, socks and lab coat, and began scrubbing his exposed skin with antiseptic soap.

"Washing's no use." Laura leaned weakly against

the counter. "You've already inhaled the virus. Antiseptic won't help."

In shock, Wayne turned, slid to the floor in a crouch and sat, hugging his knees. Kyle ignored him and raced to Laura.

"The virus works fast," she said with an apologetic smile. "I can't stay on my feet much longer."

Kyle swept her into his arms, then sat on the lab floor and cradled her against his chest. He refused to admit they were dying, in spite of what she'd told Pritchard. The other scientists would come for them. There had to be an antidote. Laura had made him want to live again after the tragedies in his life. She had bonded with Molly, becoming the mother his little girl so desperately needed. He couldn't lose her now that he'd come to love her so deeply. They could overcome their differences, their misunderstandings.

But he couldn't overcome death.

He wanted to throw back his head and howl at the universe, but he contained his rage and grief, exhibiting only tenderness to the woman in his arms.

"I'm sorry." She leaned her head against his chest, and he threaded his fingers through her dark hair, defying death to take her from his grasp.

He could barely speak through the sorrow that clogged his throat. "The spill wasn't your fault."

She shook her head, and the effort seemed to take all her strength. "I'm sorry for being angry at you about investigating Daddy."

"It's okay." He could almost see the life seeping from her. "Save your strength. Don't talk."

"I have to tell you." She struggled for breath. "I understand…just doing your job. I love you."

She went slack in his arms. "No, Laura! Hang on. Stay with me. Help's on the way."

He glared at Pritchard, cringing against the counter on the other side of the room. "If she dies, I swear to you, if the virus doesn't kill you, I will."

Pritchard managed a sneer. "This stuff is lethal, man. None of us is getting out of here alive."

Behind Kyle, the double doors opened with a bang, and three figures dressed in anticontamination suits with helmets and self-contained breathing units bore down on them, reminding Kyle of extraterrestrials in an old sci-fi movie. The first person approached and bent down over Laura. Through the Plexiglas faceplate, he recognized C.J.

"What happened?" The breathing filter distorted C.J.'s voice, making it sound as scratchy and indistinct as an old record played on a bad sound system.

Kyle pointed to the broken glass in the puddle on the floor. "D-5A. It splashed over Laura. Where's the antidote?"

From the look in C.J.'s eyes, he knew the answer before she spoke.

"There *is* none. Not yet."

"But, Laura…"

The other suited figures moved C.J. aside, and Dr. Potter and Gary Bowen reached for Laura and gently lifted her from Kyle's arms.

"We're taking her to the infirmary," Potter said. He nodded to Bowen, who carried Laura out the door, then turned back to Kyle. "Can you walk?"

"I'm fine," Kyle said. "Pritchard should go to the infirmary, too, but he's not going without me. He's the one who killed Dr. Tyson."

Potter's usually friendly features hardened behind his face mask. "Maybe we should just leave him here."

Kyle pushed to his feet and shook his head. "He has information we need. I'm going with you to make sure he cooperates."

Potter's expression turned puzzled. "I can't understand why you're displaying no symptoms."

Kyle shrugged. "Maybe I have a natural immunity, but, really, I feel fine. Just worried about Laura."

Kyle crossed to Pritchard and dragged him to his feet. The lab assistant was obviously ill, bathed in sweat and shivering with fever. "Come with me," Kyle ordered.

"You have to help me," Wayne begged. "You can't let me die."

"Is that what Dr. Tyson asked just before you broke his neck?"

With Potter's help, Kyle half carried, half dragged Wayne down to the hall to the lab's infirmary. Filled with four hospital beds, the room had been designed for a contamination crisis. Its pharmacy was stocked with every known antidote to biological weapons.

Except D-5A.

C.J. set down the receiver of a telephone when Kyle and the others entered. Laura was already tucked into a hospital bed with an IV tube inserted into her arm. While Bowen and Potter placed Pritchard in a bed on the other side of the room, C.J. approached Kyle.

"I've spoken with the Centers for Disease Control in Atlanta," she said. "They're dispatching a team of specialists immediately."

"Have you given Laura the antidote?"

The scientist shook her head. "I've told you. It isn't ready. We haven't run all the testing protocols—"

"What are her chances without it?"

"We'll know better when the specialists arrive. This virus takes hours to do its worst. Right now, her symptoms are mild."

"Mild! She's so weak she can't move."

C.J. nodded. "That's a hopeful sign. Those with early onset of the virus seem to fight it off best. It's you I'm worried about."

"Me? I keep telling you, I feel fine."

"We'll let the specialists be the judge of that. Meanwhile, let me hook you up to a gamma globulin IV and antivirals to help your immune system fight this."

Kyle glanced at his watch. The Black Order's forty-eight-hour deadline was ticking away. "Can't. I have to talk to Pritchard."

C.J. shook her head. "He needs rest, and so do you."

"He's Black Order, and if I don't find out where the rest of them are hiding and what they've done with the D-5 and anthrax, thousands will be dying by this time tomorrow."

More than anything, Kyle wanted to go to Laura,

to hold her and assure her she was going to make it—that they both were going to beat this killer and build a life together with Molly. Even if that wasn't true, he wanted to spend their last hours together. But he couldn't go to her. He had a job to do.

He crossed the room to the bed where Pritchard lay shaking with chills while Potter inserted an IV in his arm. Kyle moved the scientist aside and sat on the edge of Pritchard's bed. "There's a special team en route from the CDC in Atlanta," he told Wayne.

"Thank God," Wayne managed to say through chattering teeth. "Do they have an antidote?"

"Yes," Kyle lied. "But you're not getting it."

"What? But I'm dying."

"And a horrible death it will be, too. D-5 makes Ebola look like a case of the sniffles."

Wayne struggled to raise himself on his elbows, his formerly handsome face gray and haggard. "You can't let me die. That's murder."

"Funny," Kyle said. "You haven't had a problem with murder up till now. First your buddies killed three innocent people with their bomb. Then you killed Lawrence Tyson."

"You can't prove that." Wayne coughed, fighting for breath. "You can't prove I'm connected to the Black Order."

"Maybe. Maybe not. But if you cooperate with me, I can make certain you get your share of the antidote before it's too late."

"Cooperate?" Wariness filled Wayne's brown eyes. "How?"

"Start talking. Tell me everything you know about

the Black Order—and why you killed Dr. Tyson.
Otherwise the only way you're leaving this room is
in a body bag.''

HOURS LATER, Kyle sat by Laura's bed. The CDC
specialists had arrived and examined her, but had
verified C.J.'s assessment. There was little anyone
could do without an antidote. Only time would tell
whether Laura could fight off the dreaded virus on
her own.

He felt her squeeze his hand and looked up to see
her eyes open and staring at him.

''Hi,'' she said with a weak smile.

Even as ill as she was, her extraordinary beauty
had him struggling not to cry. She was too good, too
special to die. He needed her. Molly needed her. He
tightened his grip on her fingers, unwilling to let her
go.

''Hi.'' Flashing an optimistic smile took all his
effort. ''How are you feeling?''

''Better.'' The weakness in her voice belied her
word. ''How are you?''

''No problem. No symptoms.'' He brushed a fine
strand of dark hair off her forehead. ''Don't worry
about me. Just concentrate on getting well.''

''Wayne?''

''His condition's the same as yours.''

''He's our traitor, isn't he?''

Kyle nodded. ''He killed Tyson when Tyson overheard him making a phone call to his contact in the
Black Order.''

Her eyes widened in surprise. "Wayne confessed?"

Kyle nodded. "He told us where to find the others. They're hiding out at a cabin in Upper Ford, near Eureka, right on the Canadian border. That's where they're holding Governor Haskel. Daniel, Frank, Court, the FBI, the ATF and the Canadian Mounties are going after them." He glanced at his watch. It was almost 10:00 p.m. "They should be rounding them up right about now."

She smiled, and the sweetness of it tore at his heart. He couldn't bear the thought of not seeing that smile, not hearing that voice every day for the rest of his life.

"Then the others are safe," she said.

"The others?"

"The people who would have died from the D-5 and anthrax."

He blinked back tears at her unselfishness. "The Black Order won't be killing anybody else."

A small furrow appeared between her eyebrows.

"What's wrong," he asked. "Are you in pain?"

She shook her head and smiled again with excruciating sweetness. "I was just trying to remember whether I'd told you that I love you."

"You did."

Mischief glinted in her eyes. "And did you tell me?"

He leaned forward and gathered her to him, grief tearing at his insides like a pack of ravaging wild dogs. "Oh, God, Laura, you know I love you."

Her breath caressed his ear as she spoke. ''Then everything's going to be all right.''

''Yeah.'' He choked back a sob. ''Everything's going to be fine.''

Suddenly a pain shot through his head as if someone had pounded an iron spike through his skull. He gasped and straightened, freeing Laura from his embrace.

''What's wrong?'' Laura's voice seemed to come from far away.

Kyle tried to stand but the room rotated around him. ''I don't…''

He couldn't speak. He couldn't breathe. And then his sight went dark, just before he hit the floor.

THE SENSATION OF LIGHT returned first. Kyle opened his eyes to sunlight cascading through the glass wall of the infirmary. The shutters had been lifted. He was lying in a hospital bed. The virus must have finally taken effect. He rolled his head on the pillow to catch a glimpse of Laura. Cold fear shot through him when he saw her bed empty, the linens and coverlet replaced as if she'd never been there.

He closed his eyes and fought the despair that racked him. She had lost her fight with the D-5A virus. With his grief, the light seemed to leave the room, until he realized someone had stepped between him and the windows.

He opened his eyes. Laura stood beside his bed, looking like an angel, her hair framing her lovely face like an obsidian halo, her blue eyes shining.

''How're you feeling?'' She sat beside him and cupped his cheek in her hand.

Covering her hand with his own, he turned his head to kiss her palm. Her skin was warm, vibrant beneath his lips. He had to be delirious. ''You're not dead?''

''If I were any more alive, I couldn't stand it.''

Joy shot through him like a bottle rocket. ''How?''

''You, Wayne and I were all dying. In Wayne and me, the antivirals were only slowing the progression of the disease, not curing it. The antivirals weren't helping you at all. The specialists conferred with C.J. and decided she should try her antidote, even though it hadn't been tested. Obviously, it worked.''

He breathed a silent prayer of thanks to C.J. She'd given him back his life and Laura, his reason for living. ''How long have I been like this?''

''Three days.''

''Three days! What did you tell Molly?''

''She's still at the ranch with Dale and Jewel. They told her you had a bad cold and didn't want to give it to her.''

''Is she okay?''

''Happy as a clam. Jewel and Ribbons keep her busy, but she misses you.''

''I'll have to call her—'' He glanced across the room and saw that the other bed, too, was now deserted. ''Where's Pritchard?''

A shadow flickered across her face. ''You have some visitors waiting to see you. If you feel strong enough, I'll let them tell you.''

''I'm feeling stronger by the minute.''

"Then I'll send them in."

He grabbed her hand as she rose to leave. "Don't go."

"I'll be right out in the hall." She leaned down and brushed a feathery kiss across his lips. His sudden surge of desire assured him he'd recovered.

In less than a minute, Daniel, Frank and Court, grinning as if they'd won the lottery, stood grouped around his bed.

Court gazed down at him, shook his head then spoke to Frank beside him. "Isn't that just like a greenhorn? When the action starts, he decides to put his feet up, take a little vacation."

Frank nodded, his mouth grim but his eyes glinting with humor. "Poor ole cuss. Flew to D.C., clipped a few wires and wore himself plumb out. Had to take a rest while the rest of us dodged bullets."

Their words were gruff, but Kyle could read the concern in their eyes, sense the camaraderie in their presence. Frank and Court stood shoulder to shoulder with Daniel, like the Three Musketeers. And Kyle felt like the fourth. These men had become his friends, his brothers. He could take their ribbing, knowing that if any of those bullets had come his way, any one of the Montana Confidential agents would have risked their lives for his.

All for one and one for all.

"Don't keep me in suspense, fellows," he begged. "Tell me what happened."

Daniel pulled up a chair and straddled it backward. Frank sat at the foot of Kyle's bed. Court remained on his feet, pacing off nervous energy.

"The information you got from Pritchard paid off," Daniel said. "We managed to surprise the Black Order at their hideaway. At first there was a pretty fierce firefight, but when they realized they were surrounded and outgunned, they surrendered."

"We even rescued Governor Haskel without a scratch," Court said. "He's coming by later today to thank you personally."

"And the biological weapons?" Kyle asked.

"The anthrax was hidden in a jar of mayonnaise in Pritchard's refrigerator," Daniel said, "just like he told you. He'd been waiting for an opportunity to smuggle it out to his contact."

"And the D-5 was recovered in the cabin at Upper Ford," Frank said. "We also found their plans for releasing it into the water supply at Great Falls. We got there just in time. An hour later and they'd have been on the road, on their way to deliver it."

Kyle leaned back against his pillow in relief. "So you got them all."

Court shifted uneasily from one boot to the other, and Daniel and Frank exchanged uneasy glances.

"Not exactly," Daniel said. "Their leader, Dimitri Chilton, got away."

"Into Canada?" Kyle asked.

Court shook his head. "We don't think so. We've got an all-points bulletin out on him to law enforcement across the Northwest, along with photographs. It's only a matter of time before he's picked up."

Kyle looked from one agent to the other. "Then why do all of you look like your dog just died?"

Daniel sighed. "Because Dimitri wasn't calling the shots."

"Who was?" Kyle asked.

"We don't know," Court said. "Pritchard had promised to tell us as soon as he had a lawyer. He was hoping to use the information as part of a plea bargain."

Kyle frowned. "What happened? Did he change his mind?"

Frank rubbed his knee as if his old injury pained him. "Had it changed for him. A sniper's bullet hit him when we were taking him to the van to transfer him to state prison."

"A clean shot," Daniel said. "He died instantly."

"You think Chilton was the shooter?" Kyle asked.

Daniel nodded. "Either Chilton or his boss, whoever the son of a bitch is."

Kyle raised himself on his elbows. "Where're my clothes? Looks like we still have work to do."

Daniel placed a restraining hand on his shoulder. "The doctors say you should take another day of bed rest."

"Yeah," Court said with a grin, "and you're going to need it."

"Why's that?" Kyle asked.

Frank laughed. "'Cause when you get out of here, we're going to work your butt off to make up for this little holiday."

"Plus," Court said with a wink, "there's a good-looking woman out in the hall who looks like she has plans for you herself. Could involve some *strenuous* exercise. You'd better save your strength."

After a series of hearty handshakes and claps on the back, the agents left. Kyle could hear their polite goodbyes to Laura in the hall before she entered the room.

"Come here." He opened his arms to her and she flew into them. Drawing her into a tight embrace, he tugged her onto the bed beside him. "When that vial broke over your feet in the lab, I feared you wouldn't survive it."

She nestled her head in the hollow of his neck. "I've never been so frightened."

"Of dying?"

"Of losing you."

"I love you, Laura." He grasped her shoulders and gazed into her eyes. "Marry me."

A teasing smile lifted the corners of her delectable mouth. "Been there, done that."

"I'm serious. I want us to have a wedding with Molly and our friends there, so everyone will know our marriage is the real thing, not part of my job."

Her forehead wrinkled, her mouth pursed, she said nothing, and his heart sank. Now that her mind was no longer clouded by the virus, had she changed her feelings for him?

"Well?" he insisted, then held his breath.

"I'm thinking."

"What's there to think about?"

She reached up and placed her hands on his face, meeting his gaze straight on. "How much I love you."

"Is that a yes?"

She laughed, and her voice rang through the room like music. ''That most definitely is a yes.''

''Thank God.''

''But we'll have tons of plans to make. Molly can finally be our 'f'ower girl,' and—'' She started to say more, but he stopped her with a kiss, and he didn't let her go for a long, long time.

Epilogue

Daniel stood on the front porch of the Lonesome Pony and shaded his eyes against the sun. If he squinted, he could just make out Whitney on her bay Appaloosa and Jewel on her sorrel gelding as they disappeared among the trees that lined the rocky trail into the Absaroka-Beartooth Mountains.

He was glad he'd convinced Whitney to take a break. She'd been working night and day fielding calls from law enforcement agencies all over the state, reports of sightings of Dimitri Chilton. None of the leads, however, had yet panned out. Daniel had eyed the stack of papers on her desk, the unnatural pallor of her skin and the fine lines of fatigue etched around her eyes, and prepared to issue an ultimatum.

"Nice job, Whit," he'd told her.

And he'd meant it. He'd never expected the beautiful young woman from her wealthy and well-connected family to be anything but a pain in the butt when he'd agreed to let her work at the ranch. But she'd surprised him with her competence, her stamina and her intelligence. She'd proven herself an important asset to the Montana Confidential team.

"Now take a break," he'd ordered.

She'd waved her hand at a stack of reports. "But—"

"Don't argue. You'll work more efficiently after a break. It's a gorgeous day. Enjoy it."

She'd taken his advice when Jewel had invited Whitney for a trail ride.

The screen door behind him opened and shut, and Dale appeared at his side with a mug of steaming coffee and handed it to him. She glanced toward the trail where Whitney and Jewel had headed up the mountain, then turned back to him. "You should take your own advice. You're working too hard."

"Dimitri Chilton's still out there. We have to find him."

"Hmmph. Finding him can't be all that critical. You sent Kyle off on a honeymoon."

"He needed the rest. He was itching to get back on the case, but the doctors said both he and Laura should take it easy. Their bodies are still fighting off the aftereffects of that D-5A."

"Drink your coffee," she ordered in the gruff way she had of taking care of him. "Put your feet up for fifteen minutes and ease your mind. Like you told Whitney, you'll be the better for it."

He smiled at the woman who was not only his housekeeper but his friend. "Thanks, Dale. Grab a cup and join me. You work too hard, yourself. You knocked yourself out on that wedding reception for Kyle and Laura. Never saw such a great spread."

"No rest for the wicked," she said with a grin. "But I'm glad to keep busy. I miss that little 'un."

She knuckled away a tear with a work-roughened hand and went back inside.

Taking her advice, Daniel settled in a rocker and propped his boots on the porch railing. He missed Molly, too. She'd been a ray of sunshine in all their lives, but this morning she'd flown out with Kyle and Laura. They would drop her off at Kyle's parents' in California before heading to Acapulco for their honeymoon.

Daniel thought back to the ceremony at the little A-frame church in Paradise Valley yesterday. Laura had wanted to keep the wedding simple out of respect to her father's recent passing, but it had been a moving event, nonetheless. Laura had been radiant in her simple but elegant white gown, and Kyle, though still pale from his illness, had looked as handsome as Daniel had ever seen him.

Daniel smiled, remembering Molly in her ruffled yellow dress, carrying her basket of rose petals. Blond curls bouncing, green eyes sparkling and her tongue set carefully in the corner of her mouth, she had carefully allotted the blossoms as she'd come down the aisle, only to find her basket half-full when she reached the altar. Without breaking her stride, she'd dumped the rest of the petals in a pile at the minister's feet. Daniel had thought he'd bust a gut to keep from laughing.

But everyone had laughed and applauded later in the ceremony, when the minister had asked Kyle if he would love, honor and keep Laura. "I will," Kyle had answered solemnly.

"Me, too," Molly had piped in.

Daniel sipped his coffee and thought back to another wedding, another bride. He and Sherry had been so much in love, so full of hopes and dreams, but the anxiety, stress and pressures of his job had formed a wedge between them. Somehow it had all gone wrong.

But it doesn't have to stay that way, an inner voice reminded him.

With a sigh of satisfaction, he realized that maybe, just maybe, he'd have another shot at building a life with Sherry. She and Jessie would be arriving for a visit soon. God, it would be good to have them under the same roof again. Who knew, maybe this time, he could work things out—

He jerked up his head at the sound of shouting at the far edge of the pasture. Jewel, hatless and screaming at the top of her lungs, was riding her aging gelding hell-for-leather toward the ranch.

Alone.

Daniel jumped to his feet and ran to meet her.

"Whitney," he heard her screaming as she approached. "You gotta help Whitney!"

She drew the lathered horse to a stop when she reached him and jumped down into his arms.

"Is Whitney hurt?" he asked.

Jewel shook her head and gasped for breath. "Some guy grabbed her up on the trail. She's been kidnapped."

You've read the first three books of

MONTANA CONFIDENTIAL.

Now don't miss the exciting conclusion,

> *SECRET AGENT HEIRESS*
> *by Julie Miller*

Available next month wherever
Harlequin Intrigues are sold.

For a special preview of

SECRET AGENT HEIRESS,

Turn the page...
and let the excitement
and passion begin!

Chapter One

"I'm not dead."

The observation squeaked through the parched ache in Whitney's throat as she woke up. She tried to reach up to massage the bruised tissue at her neck, but a rough reminder pinched the skin at her wrist.

She breathed in stale, undisturbed air and opened her eyes to the dim morning light before remembering the source of the pain. Several layers of wide gray duct tape bound her wrists to the arms of a warped hardwood chair.

But knowledge didn't necessarily bring comfort. Like a condemned woman strapped in for a primitive electrocution, her wrists and ankles had been taped to the arms and legs of her chair. She had no fear of being electrocuted, though. The ramshackle, one-room cabin where she'd spent the night hadn't seen electricity or running water for years—if ever.

She breathed in deeply and winced at the burning in her chest. Combined with the rapid pounding inside her head, her achy body felt as if she'd been hit by a Mack truck...or thrown from her horse...or...

"Good morning, Miss MacNair."

Whitney's senses snapped to full alert at the crisply articulated greeting. The man in black.

Dimitri Chilton.

He lounged across the room from her in a battered recliner upholstered with ratty, mildewed plaid. With one leg draped carelessly over the arm of the chair, the front of his wool coat gaped open, revealing the steel-gray butt of an oversize handgun sticking out of a holster beneath his left arm.

She'd attacked a man carrying that kind of fire-power? Even the Department of Public Safety agents who worked at Montana Confidential didn't walk around wearing weapons that looked like some sort of handheld mini cannon. The pockets of her jeans held nothing more dangerous than a tube of lip balm and a tissue.

Her pulse rate kicked up a notch. He could have killed her on the spot with that thing. He could have brought down Jewel McMurty and both horses, too. God, she was an idiot. No wonder her parents and brothers, and the men she worked with, thought she couldn't look after herself.

With very little effort, she'd made a mess of things again.

A flash of white teeth in the shadows, and the be-mused laugh that accompanied the smile, brought her back to the present. Whitney forced herself to breathe calmly, in and out through her nose.

Second-guessing herself now wouldn't help. She had to keep a clear head. She dredged up the stiff-lipped pride that had seen her through tough times before. She refused to bend her spirit to her captor, even though he clearly had the upper hand.

"Where are we? What time is it?" She squinted through the shadows, trying to bring his face into focus. "Have you called my father yet? I know who you are."

"I know you as well." His crisp Mediterranean accent bespoke a man of education and culture. But the bruises on her body gave testament to his penchant for violence. "Your father will be contacted when the time is right. He paid good money to silence your embarrassing little scandal, no? You were whisked away from an important job in Washington to become a ranch hand in Montana. And you had such a promising career ahead of you."

Whitney withered at the false sympathy lacing his voice. So much for pride. Even a terrorist from the other side of the world had heard of the pampered rich girl's shame. "So you read the newspapers, too."

"I wouldn't be doing my job very well if I wasn't informed, now, would I. I must make sure your father wants you back before I ask for ransom money."

Chilton had hit her at her most vulnerable spot. For the moment, she conceded victory to him.

"Then what do you want with me?"

He slowly unhooked his leg from the chair and leaned forward into the dusty shaft of sunlight streaming in through a lone, cracked windowpane. Dark, intelligent eyes studied her with superior indifference. She relished a brief satisfaction at seeing the dark purple blotches beneath both those eyes.

She'd broken the bastard's nose with one of those kicks yesterday.

But satisfaction was brief. Something about his unblinking stare made her suddenly conscious of how vulnerable she was.

"You are my ticket to freedom and…revenge."

"What?" For a few breathless seconds, she pitied whoever had been foolish enough to cross him. He spoke so matter-of-factly, as if he had already planned his enemy's death a thousand times, in a thousand different ways.

And then she began to wonder just who his target for revenge might be. Montana Confidential? Her family?

Whitney sank back into her chair, unable to ward off the chill that assailed her. Every bruise and scrape on her back and arms cried out, each wound a tiny little voice reminding her of who she was and what she was supposed to be. Gerald MacNair's little girl. She was simply a pawn in this madman's game. Not Whitney. Not a woman. Not even a human being.

A pawn.

'TIS THE SEASON FOR...

HARLEQUIN®
INTRIGUE®

Fill your Christmas stocking with
two new seasonal tales of breathtaking
romantic suspense from a couple
of your favorite authors.

ANOTHER WOMAN'S BABY
Joanna Wayne
(11/01)

A WOMAN WITH A MYSTERY
B.J. Daniels
(12/01)

Available at your favorite retail outlet.

HARLEQUIN®
Makes any time special ®

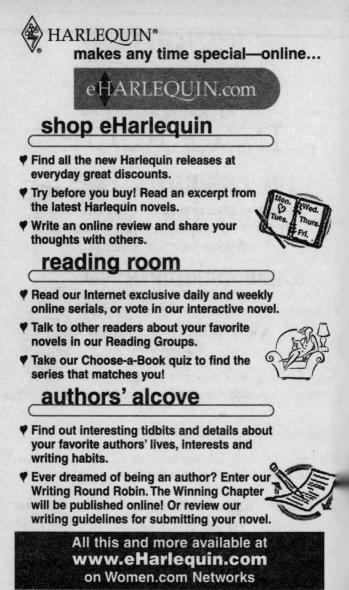

TRUEBLOOD, TEXAS

Coming in December 2001…

THE COWBOY'S SECRET SON

by

Gayle Wilson

Lost:

His first love. Mark Peterson had never forgotten Jillian Salvini, whose family had left town in the middle of the night so many years ago.

Found:

Her son's father. Jillian has finally returned… with her son, Drew, who bears an uncanny resemblance to Jillian's next-door neighbor: Mark Peterson!

Can old wounds and past betrayals be overcome, so that Mark, Jillian and Drew can finally become a family?

Finder's Keepers: bringing families together

HARLEQUIN®

Makes any time special ®

 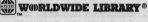

HARLEQUIN®
INTRIGUE®

43 Light St.

has been *the* address for outstanding romantic suspense for more than a decade! Now REBECCA YORK* blasts the hinges off the front door with a new trilogy— MINE TO KEEP.

Look for these great stories on the corner of heart-stopping romance and breathtaking suspense!

THE MAN FROM TEXAS
August 2001

NEVER ALONE
October 2001

LASSITER'S LAW
December 2001

COME ON OVER...
WE'LL KEEP THE LIGHTS ON.

Available at your favorite retail outlet.

*Ruth Glick writing as Rebecca York

AND YOU THOUGHT TEXAS WAS BIG!

HARLEQUIN®
INTRIGUE®

continues its most secret, seriously sinister and deadly *confidential* series in the Big Sky state with four more sexy cowboy agents guaranteed to take your breath away!

Men bound by love, loyalty and the law— these specialized government operatives have vowed to keep their missions and identities confidential....

SOMEONE TO PROTECT HER
PATRICIA ROSEMOOR
September 2001

SPECIAL ASSIGNMENT: BABY
DEBRA WEBB
October 2001

LICENSED TO MARRY
CHARLOTTE DOUGLAS
November 2001

SECRET AGENT HEIRESS
JULIE MILLER
December 2001

Available wherever Harlequin books are sold.

HARLEQUIN®
Makes any time special®